Lure of the Fox

Book 6
Aloha Shifters: Jewels of the Heart

by Anna Lowe

TWIN MOON PRESS

Editing by Lisa A. Hollett

Covert art by Kim Killion

Contents

Other books in this series

Aloha Shifters - Jewels of the Heart

Lure of the Dragon (Book 1)

Lure of the Wolf (Book 2)

Lure of the Bear (Book 3)

Lure of the Tiger (Book 4)

Love of the Dragon (Book 5)

Lure of the Fox (Book 6)

visit www.annalowebooks.com

Free Books

Get your free e-books now!

Sign up for my newsletter at *annalowebooks.com* to get three free books!

- *Desert Wolf*: Friend or Foe (Book 1.1 in the Twin Moon Ranch series)

- *Off the Charts* (the prequel to the Serendipity Adventure series)

- *Perfection* (the prequel to the Blue Moon Saloon series)

Chapter One

Jake raised his fist and knocked on the massive gate at the end of the private drive. Then he stepped back and crossed his arms to wait, studying the swirly design carved into the wood. At first, he thought it was a toothy lizard, but then he spotted the wings.

He shaded his eyes from the tropical sun and checked again. A dragon?

He'd heard rumors about the guys of Special Forces OD-X unit — rumors that their amazing feats and incredible power came from some not-quite-human side. He'd never believed that nonsense, because he knew firsthand what the human body could do when a man went into survival mode.

He stared into the eyes of the carved dragon. Heroes, he could believe in. But supernatural heroes? He'd never believed that bullshit.

But for a flicker of an instant, he wasn't so sure. Of course, these days, it was hard to be sure about anything. His eyes darted over the thick foliage surrounding the quiet lane, and his hands reached for the weapon he no longer carried. Then he cursed and rolled his shoulders a few times. Damn it, he'd been stateside for nearly two months. This wasn't a war zone. So why were his nerves always on high alert?

Possibly because the massive wooden gate screamed *Private! Danger!* and *Keep out!* Or possibly because he was more used to breaching walls and scaling fences than waiting to be let in.

He banged three more times and called out. "Hello?"

Nothing. No reaction. Crickets.

1

Then the bushes rustled, and a calico kitten tiptoed along the top of the gate, purring at him. Jake chuckled. So much for rumors of men who vanished, leaving ferocious wild animals in their place.

"Hey, little guy." He held out a hand.

The kitten sniffed the air and flicked its tricolor tail.

"Let me guess. You're head of security," Jake quipped. "No wonder they need help."

The fur ball gave a plaintive meow, prompting Jake to pet it. It had thick, healthy fur, unlike some of the sorry strays Jake used to throw scraps to in various war-torn parts of the world.

"You reckon I'm in the right place?" he asked.

The kitten closed its eyes and purred under Jake's touch as he squinted at the gate. There wasn't actually a plaque labeled *Koa Point Estate*, but the place matched the description provided by his friend, Boone Hawthorne. Of course, it was hard to tell when Boone was joking and when the guy was serious. Maybe Boone had been bullshitting about living on an oceanfront estate.

A whirring sound came from overhead, and Jake snapped his head up and crouched, arms out, fists balled, ready for action. The kitten skittered into the bushes, spooked.

"Damn it." That was just a security camera, not a band of hidden insurgents turning their weapons on him. No reason at all for his heart rate to spike and sweat to break out over his brow.

"Hello?" a gritty voice growled. "Who is it?"

Jake glared at the intercom hidden behind huge leaves. "McBride, reporting for duty."

The growl turned into a friendly cackle that could only belong to Boone Hawthorne. "Jake! You found us."

"Sure did."

"Well, come in already." A click sounded, and the gate slowly slid to one side. "I'll meet you on the way down."

Jake readjusted his backpack and stepped forward, wondering what to expect. The kitten reappeared and wound between his legs, slowing him down.

"You live here too?" Jake asked. A second later, he stepped past the thick hedge and whistled. "Wow. Lucky kitty."

The cat blinked up at him, wide-eyed, innocent, and blissfully unaware of how most of the world's population lived.

A stand of trees gave way to a manicured, putting-green lawn dotted with beds of exotic flowers. The smooth driveway curved around stands of old-growth forest where leaves whispered in the sea breeze. None of it resembled anything like what he'd grown up with in Colorado, and definitely not like anything he'd seen on four successive tours of duty that had taken him to so many forgotten corners of the globe.

"Jake!" A sandy-haired man strode into view — barefoot, bare-chested, clad in nothing but a colorful sarong.

Yep, that was definitely Boone Hawthorne. Jake had only ever seen the guy in fatigues, but even then, Boone's sunny surfer side had shone through. But what the hell was he doing on a ritzy estate like this?

"Holy shit, Boone. Did you inherit a couple of million or rob a bank?"

Boone grinned and pulled Jake into a back-smacking man-hug. "No inheritance, no heists. Me and the guys just happened to land the sweetest caretaking deal in the islands."

For once, Boone wasn't kidding. The garage Jake spotted around the next turn had space for at least a dozen cars, and a shiny red Ferrari stood parked outside one of the bays.

When the kitten swiped at the trailing edge of Boone's sarong, Boone scooped it up and nuzzled it with his chin. "I see Keiki has already introduced herself." Then he stopped and smacked Jake on the shoulder again. "I can't believe you're here. So good to see you, man."

"Good to see you too." Jake grinned.

It had been nearly eighteen months since he'd last seen Boone, sometime after the three missions their units had co-operated on. But right away, it felt like old times. Most of all, it felt good to see someone he wouldn't have to explain anything to. Like why a mess kit had to be kept clean or why he kept his gear packed in such tight, neat folds. Why he sometimes woke up in a cold sweat.

"The guys will be glad to see you too," Boone said.

"Your whole unit is here?"

"Yep. Me, Hunter, and Cruz — when he's not off somewhere with his mate—" Boone stuttered a little, then went on. "Housemate. I mean, his girlfriend. Kai and Silas are here too."

Jake followed him, trying to process it all. Swaying palm trees. A strip of aquamarine water off what seemed to be a private beach. Boone hadn't been kidding when he said *sweet*. And wow, the whole unit was still together. Jake was still in touch with his buddies, but they'd all gone separate ways. Which would have been fine if he knew they were all off pursuing their own definitions of happiness — but, no. Junger had been killed in a climbing accident, and Chalsmith died in a car crash, both within the last few weeks. It pained Jake to think about all the risks they'd taken in war zones, only to die when they got home. Hoover, another member of his unit, had even muttered something about reenlisting to live a safer life.

Jake, on the other hand, had put the army firmly behind him once his honorable discharge had gone through. He'd headed home, given his mom his Distinguished Service Cross, and put out feelers for jobs. And of all people, Boone Hawthorne — a guy who might have been named *most likely to turn into a beach bum* — had been the first to write back.

"Sorry to hear about your guys," Boone murmured as if he'd picked up on Jake's thoughts.

"Yeah. Thanks." Jake cleared his throat. "And thanks for writing about the job."

"Your timing was perfect." Boone gestured around. "We were looking for a couple of extra security guards when you wrote, and everyone agreed you'd be perfect. We figured Maui would appeal too."

Maui had sounded great, and security guard was fine with him, especially since he hadn't been able to turn off the hypervigilant part of his mind. Maybe a few months in this job would help him settle down. And who knew? It might even help him forget the woman he couldn't get out of his mind.

4

You're meant for each other, a little voice in the back of his mind said. *She is your destiny.*

He kicked the grass path. That had been nearly eighteen months back, but his mind insisted on replaying the memories over and over again.

Memories of the coolest, most collected woman he'd ever met. One with reddish-blond hair, piercing brown-orange eyes, and thin, no-nonsense lips. *Petite* didn't suit a woman with that much attitude, and the tattoos etched into her arms only heightened the effect. All the men she'd worked with refrained from saying *five-foot-two* and called her *six-foot-minus-ten* instead. Ella rarely let her feminine side show, but when they'd been alone, she'd given him everything for one scorching, unforgettable night.

A black bird with a yellow mask swooped over his head, and *poof!* Those memories of Ella vanished with that bandit of a bird, leaving him blinking upward.

Boone was gesturing toward the ocean and saying something, but Jake missed most of it. "Over there... private beach... helipad..."

Jake shook his head, telling himself he wasn't in love. That one torrid night didn't mean forever. It was probably one of those weird things war had knocked into his head. Now that he was back — a free man, no longer bound to take orders from anyone — he'd get over Ella and go back to living the nice, simple life of a bachelor. Like that line in some poem, he'd be the captain of his own destiny. No complications, no one to tie him down.

"This is our meeting house," Boone said as they approached a thatch-roofed building with open sides where several men stood. "You remember Hunter, right?"

Jake grasped Hunter's outstretched hand and shook it heartily. How could he forget the giant, lumberjack type? "Good to see you."

They shook warmly until something orange flashed between them, making Hunter laugh.

"Whoa there, Keiki," he murmured to the kitten, who perched happily on his shoulder, purring.

"Got yourself a real tiger there." Jake chuckled.

"Ha. She wishes," Boone laughed.

Someone giggled. Hunter raised one bushy eyebrow, and even the kitten seemed to wink.

Jake looked around. What was that about?

"Hi." A friendly blonde stepped forward with a warm smile. "I'm Nina. So nice to meet you."

Jake moved his lips, a little lost for words when Boone slid an arm around the woman's waist — her very full, bulging waist. Apparently, Boone had found himself a nice woman and was the proud father-to-be of a child who couldn't be too far from being born. More proof that life didn't stand still, even if it sometimes felt that way in the time he'd been away.

"You'll get to meet the twins pretty soon." Boone grinned from ear to ear.

"Congratulations," Jake managed, still surprised. Boone, of all people...

"You know Kai. And this is Tessa," Boone continued.

"Hi," a striking redhead said.

Jake shook hands with her and got a solid shoulder smack from Kai, who grinned. Jake did too. So many familiar faces, all of them obviously doing well. Settled down and happily partnered up, from the look of it.

"So who else do you know? Oh — Cruz." Boone waved toward a thick stand of trees on the far side of the property. "He's prowling around somewhere — or surfing with Jody."

Jake's eyebrows shot up. Cruz was a surly, leave-me-alone kind of guy, and prowling fit perfectly. But surfing? No way.

"Silas and Cassandra will be back from New York in a week," Boone finished, looking around. "I guess that's everyone." Hunter growled — really growled — and Boone hastened to add, "And Dawn! You can meet her tonight."

Jake found his pulse skipping faster. If all the men of the OD-X unit were here, maybe Ella was too.

But, no. He'd heard Ella was in Arizona, and a good thing too. He was trying to forget her, not to throw oil on a smoldering fire.

"So, what have you been up to?" Boone asked.

Jake's mind went blank. The past weeks were a dull blur, and his only real desire — driving obsession? — had been to find Ella. Which he wasn't about to do. They'd agreed to keep it to one night and one night only for lots of good reasons he was tired of explaining to his heart. So he'd been couch-surfing from friend to friend while searching for a decent job. Something like what he'd grown up doing, working on the family ranch in Colorado. Unfortunately, that wasn't an option now that his older brother had inherited the place and rehired all the working hands he needed.

"Not really sure." Jake looked at his feet.

"Yeah," Kai murmured. "I remember that."

And for a minute, every man stared silently into the distance, lost in his own thoughts. It was only when the women quietly stepped closer that each of the men brightened and looked up again.

"The good thing is, it wears off," Kai said when Tessa touched his shoulder.

Jake shifted from foot to foot, ready to change the subject. He looked around and counted in his mind. These men — and women — were a formidable force in their own right. Why did they need an extra body to keep an eye on the place?

"What can you tell me about the job?"

Boone laughed. "Right to work, huh? We knew you'd be perfect."

Kai nodded in approval. "It's a fairly straightforward security job, keeping an eye on this estate and the adjoining property. Almost boring compared to what you're used to."

"Boring sounds good," Jake joked. "Who owns this place?"

"Let's just say he's a very private man," Boone said, exchanging knowing glances with Kai. Hunter hid a little smile, while Tessa quickly turned to face the kitchen, making Jake wonder what the joke was. Or was that just him imagining things?

"Exactly. A very private man whose businesses keep him busy all over the world," Kai added. "Which means life can be pretty quiet here most of the time. But he has enemies too, so..." His voice dropped to a menacing growl and trailed off.

The sea breeze wavered a little. Boone's face went serious — dead serious — as he squeezed Nina closer to his side. Kai bristled, and a ripple of foreboding went through the air.

Jake looked around. He'd witnessed that before — that hint of something different and dangerous about this group of men. Kai, Boone, and Hunter were all big, burly, and intense. So intense, they intimidated even the most battle-hardened soldiers with their brooding natures and undercurrent of power. Everything about them hinted at some huge, hidden secret. What that might be, he had no clue. But he did know that his friends were utterly reliable, honorable soldiers, legendary for getting impossible jobs done. He'd seen the proof firsthand.

A moment later, that hitch in the conversation passed, and Kai picked up again. "So it's critical not to let anything lull you into a false sense of security."

Jake nearly laughed out loud. "Not an issue. What's the schedule?"

"Eight-hour rotations shared with us — except Boone, whose head is too submerged in babyland to be useful. But then again, since when was Boone ever useful?" Kai laughed.

"Yeah." Boone gave a bored sigh. "I guess saving your sorry ass that time in Nangarhar doesn't count."

Kai waved a hand like that was nothing and went on. "So we, minus Big Daddy here, run all the patrols, along with you. Oh, and one other new hire."

Jake tilted his head. New hire?

Kai chuckled. "I know what you're thinking. We know how important trust is. That's why we hired you — and only one other person. You should feel honored, man."

"You're the perfect man for the job — and so is she. Even if she's not a man." Boone grinned.

Jake froze. She?

Brisk footsteps sounded behind him, and alarms went off in Jake's mind. His heart pounded in one of those *oh, shit* moments he'd experienced in combat — or more accurately, in the split second before an explosive detonated and the shit hit the fan.

"Perfect timing," Tessa called out. "Lunch is ready, and you can meet Jake."

The even stride broke off abruptly. "Meet who?"

"Aw, come on. You know Jake, right?" Boone banged him on the shoulder and motioned toward the newcomer.

Jake turned slowly, totally tongue-tied. This wasn't happening. It couldn't be.

But if there was one thing he had learned in Ranger training, it was that *not possible* could sneak up on a man at the least auspicious times.

"Ella," he said, making sure to keep his voice even. But his cheeks heated, and his blood rushed.

"Jake," Ella replied in an equally measured tone. Her mesmerizing eyes — brown with an outer ring of dark orange — were sparkling. Shooting off tiny fireworks. Practically glowing, in fact. But Ella's face remained stony, her posture rigid.

Jake stuck his hand out and they shook, stiff as a couple of marionettes.

A rush of heated images flashed through his mind. Like her dropping the tough-guy act and kissing him. Her fingers moving over his clothes, divesting him of fifteen pounds of combat gear before stripping him to the skin. Letting him do the same to her, and...

Just for tonight, she'd insisted.

Just for tonight, he'd readily agreed.

Round one had been hot and frenzied as they finally unleashed the desire that had built between them over the week since they'd met while their units shared duties. Round two had been slow and sweet, leaving Jake with a strange sense of peace. Rounds three and four were a blur, but he remembered the *after* clearly. Ella had stared at him as if stunned by some monumental truth, and he had the sense of something way, way out of his control lurching into motion.

Immediately after that night, their units had parted ways, and the two times they had crossed paths after that, Jake's heart had just about thumped right out of his chest. Ella's whole face would light up too, but then she would slap an impassive mask on and ignore him again.

Which was fine. Perfect. He didn't want more either.

So why was he holding his breath? Why did she still occupy his dreams?

"Good to see you," he said, taking her in.

God, she was something. Bristling and tough as ever. Maybe even more so, especially given the way she glared at him now. She had *don't fuck with me* written all over — practically coded into the swirling tattoo she had etched around one forearm — and the same tight, hard physique as always. Same coppery-blond hair, though it wasn't winched back into a bun any more. She wore it in a loose ponytail that still swung with her broken-off stride, mesmerizing him. Would the strands be as silky to run his hands through as they had all that time ago? Would they catch the lights like a halo if she straddled his hips and rode him like a cowgirl one more time?

"Good to see you," Ella said in clipped, cool syllables.

For a second, they got stuck there, holding hands, gazing into each other's eyes. The quiet scratch of palm fronds faded away, as did the distant sound of ocean crashing into rocks. Nothing but Ella seemed to matter — until she yanked her hand away, stepped back, and blinked.

"You remember Jake, right?" Boone said.

Ella nodded curtly. "Oh, I remember, all right."

Chapter Two

Ella forced her knees not to shake as she strode to the kitchen area of the meeting house. On the outside, she stayed perfectly composed, but on the inside...

It's him! It's him! Her inner fox jumped and cried.

Her cheeks heated, and she bit her lip as locked-away emotions came rushing back. The anguish of leaving Jake after their night together had never really faded; she'd just hidden it behind a mental wall. Turning her back on her destined mate had been the hardest thing she'd ever done. Harder than Ranger training. Harder than the toughest assignment she'd carried out as special adjunct to Silas's elite shifter unit. Harder than—

She banged her fists against her hips a few times. She'd done what she had to do, and for good reason. The question was, what the hell was Jake doing here? Boone had mentioned finding someone to help patrol Koa Point, but she had no idea it was *him.*

Jake McBride. Six solid feet of hulking cowboy-turned-soldier with chocolate-brown hair and honest blue eyes. Eyes that went soul-deep and made her want to do backflips every time he looked at her and every time he smiled, making the tiny little scar on his upper lip stretch.

She set a mug under the coffee machine and smacked the button for a double espresso. Steam hissed as she closed her eyes.

This could not be happening. She'd answered her shifter friends' call for help and come to Maui for a few weeks until a permanent security force could be hired. The shifters of Koa Point were eager to spend more time with their mates, but the ever-present threat of enemy incursion hung over the pack like a cloud. Drax, their bitter enemy, had recently been eliminated, but Moira, a vengeful she-dragon, was still on the loose — as was the Keystone, the last of a collection of precious stones with magical powers.

Boone turned to Jake. "Like I said, you wrote at the perfect time. We really need someone we know and trust."

Ella did her best not to mutter under her breath. Boone expected her to work alongside the one man she had to avoid?

"Damn lucky thing, too," Boone continued. "I never check that email address any more. I'm not really sure why I did."

"Maybe it was destiny," Nina chirped, upbeat as ever.

Ella scowled into a coffee cup. If that was true, destiny was out to torture her. Why else would it match her with a human she couldn't allow herself to love? Why would destiny bring him back to her again and again? She'd had to endure seeing Jake several times after their night together — the night that was supposed to get him out of her system — and now, destiny had steered him back to her once again.

Of course fate is bringing him to us, her fox cried. *He's our mate!*

The coffee was scalding, but she sipped it anyway. *We can't love him.*

How can we not love him? her fox demanded.

She swallowed away a sigh. Jake's clear blue eyes and guarded smile had won her over from the start. The instant, unassuming respect. The way Jake could go from uncompromising soldier to conscientious good guy when he crouched to put little kids at ease. His ability to joke away the worst meals, the lumpiest bedding, the most miserable weather. The way he would stare off into the distance as he talked about the place he called home.

He'd never demanded anything of her, only given. Things that truly mattered, like respect. Time. Space.

"You two are perfect for the job," Boone said.

We are perfect, her fox sighed.

They were perfect — in every way but one. He was a human. She was a shifter. A fox who liked to roam around at

12

dawn and dusk, sniffing the breeze. What would Jake think of that?

Ella looked at all the happy couples in the room, trying not to frown. Male shifters had it easy. It didn't matter whether a male's destined mate was human or shifter because a mating bite would bind them together forever. Their partners would gain the ability to shift, and that was that. Happily ever after.

The metabolism of a human male, on the other hand, resisted the change set off by a mating bite. The stronger the man, the harder his body fought the change, as if it were a disease. The process was more likely to kill such a man than change him — or make him lose his mind.

Ella fingered the silver chain around her neck and winced as an echo of the past whispered through her mind. A man's voice, low and determined.

I can do it. I know I'll be okay. Love will see me through this.

Ella shook her head, wishing she could go back in time and warn that man — Brian, the man her mother loved. Ella's biological father had been another desert fox who'd hooked up with her mother when they were both too young. He'd taken off before ever finding out Ella was on the way, and her mom had raised her alone. Things were fine that way, too, but life had gotten even better when Brian came along. The sweetest, kindest human who had taken Ella in like his own.

Our love will overcome, her mother had mumbled over and over as she held a wet cloth to his feverish brow. And little Ella looked on, terrified, powerless to help.

Don't worry, sweetie, Brian had said. *Destiny made your mom and me mates. It will see us through this.*

Ella stared off into the distance. Destiny didn't always hold up its end of the deal, and love didn't always overcome. Brian had died a painful death, and her mother had succumbed to grief not long after, leaving Ella alone.

She fingered her silver necklace — a gift from Brian to her mother a long time ago. Loving Jake meant resisting Jake. It was better for them both that way.

What use is a human security guard? she protested, shooting the words into her friends' minds as all closely bonded shifters could.

Jake is the next best thing, Kai said immediately. *The man has the best eyes and ears of any human I know. You know how capable he is.*

Her inner fox went warm all over at the unintended innuendo. Oh, she knew how *capable* Jake was, all right.

And until we can find more shifters we can trust, he'll be a big help patrolling the area, Kai said.

Her eyes slid over to where Jake stood in the shade of the meeting house. The average onlooker would only see *chiseled warrior* or *strapping ranch hand,* but Ella saw past that the same way Jake had always had X-ray vision for the real her. There was more than an elite soldier in his soul. A passionate, burning soul hidden as thoroughly as she concealed her own.

Want him, her fox whined. *Need him.*

If it had been nighttime, she would have shifted into fox form, raised her thin muzzle, and howled her sorrow to the moon. But it was broad daylight in Hawaii, not midnight in the desert. And if she really cared about Jake, she would keep him safe — and that meant staying away from him.

"We've got a roomy place for you to stay," Boone said to Jake, motioning over his shoulder. "The plantation house at Koakea — the neighboring property."

Ella's jaw dropped, and she almost flapped both hands at Boone in a frantic no.

"Koakea?" Jake murmured.

"It means white koa — a type of tree," Boone explained.

"Wait," Ella blurted. *She* was staying at Koakea. "That won't work."

Boone tilted his head. Hunter raised a bushy eyebrow. Jake looked at her, not judging, not protesting, just waiting to hear her out.

"What won't work?" Boone asked.

Jake and me under the same roof, she nearly said. She'd end up caving in to desire as she had once before, and that would only make it harder to fight fate.

"I think he'd be much more comfortable in the guesthouse here," she tried.

Boone shrugged. "You were the one who said it was better for the security detail to keep a certain distance, right?

She clenched her mug harder, biting her tongue. Most of the time, Boone tuned out everything but his mate's needs and last-minute preparations for his any-day-now twins. Why did he have to remember her saying that?

"The plantation house makes sense," Hunter agreed. "It's closer to our weak side."

She wanted to stamp her foot and scream. The others knew her better than anyone — so why weren't they picking up on her alarm? She, Hunter, and Kai had grown up together in a foster home run by an owl shifter named Georgia Mae. The two were like brothers to her — *hānai* brothers, as Hawaiian tradition called it.

Brothers she was sometimes tempted to kick in the shins.

"The plantation was abandoned for so long, we had problems with squatters and developers," Kai explained to Jake. "So the more people we have establishing a presence, the better."

Ella rolled her eyes. She'd been the one to point that out when she'd arrived for duty two weeks earlier. Admittedly, she'd mainly done so as an excuse to gain some distance from the others. The guys of Koa Point were comrades she would always feel bonded to, and the women they'd found were each fantastic, worthy partners in their own right. But it was hard being the odd one out in a community of shifters so starry-eyed with love they could barely see straight. Calling in outside help for security was a smart move, and housing that help at Koakea made sense too.

Except, of course, now that the help was Jake.

She crossed her arms over her chest. "The roof leaks."

Kai furrowed his brow. "You said it was fine."

"I was being polite," she growled.

Jake's eyes lit as he made the connection that she was staying there. The man had always read her better than anyone else.

15

Boone snorted. "Ha. Ella, being polite."

She glared. "There's no running water."

"No problem." Jake shrugged.

"We did install that high-tech compostable latrine," Boone said. "You said it was fine."

"You said you've seen worse," Kai pointed out. "Solar shower and all that."

Damn it, was no one getting the point?

Tessa, bless her, seemed to be the first to clue in. "Maybe Jake would be more comfortable at the guesthouse."

Ella wasn't big on hugs, but she could have smothered Tessa with gratitude for that one.

But Jake, damn him, just shrugged. "I'm sure I've seen worse."

Damn it, there he went with his mixed messages again. His stiff handshake had hinted that he would have been happy to avoid seeing her, but the way his throat bobbed when he looked at her said, *Maybe we should give it one more try.*

"You've definitely seen worse. Remember that night we spent in that gorge?" Boone said.

Ella dragged her hands through her hair. That was so not the point.

"Plus, you can coordinate your shifts better," Hunter said, scratching the kitten under the chin.

Oh, we could coordinate, all right, her fox agreed in a sultry hum.

Ella wanted to scream. She needed to coordinate some escape from this mess was more like it.

"Maybe Ella would like some privacy," Tessa said in a carefully neutral tone.

Ella was not only going to hug Tessa next time she had the chance — she'd kiss her too.

But Boone just flapped a hand. "Ella doesn't need privacy. In fact, she was always the one insisting that shared barracks were fine."

"Yeah," Kai said.

"Yeah," Hunter nodded.

Ella made a face. Those two, she was definitely kicking in the shins.

"Well, that was in the army. This is what we call civilian life. Would you like me to cook the kind of food you ate back then?" Tessa asked.

"Hell no," Boone and Kai said at the same time.

"Heck no," Hunter, ever the polite one, said.

Nina patted her bulging belly and shot the first two a *mind-your-language-around-the-babies* look.

"Sorry, honey," Boone said. "The point is, we like Tessa's cooking. No, we *love* Tessa's cooking." He turned to Jake with a serious nod. "Just wait till you try her steak."

"Or honey-coconut pancakes..." Hunter added, licking his lips.

Kai's face grew dreamy. "Or her grilled *laulau*..."

Tessa stuck up her hand in a stop sign. "The point is, you do things differently now. Maybe Ella would appreciate having some privacy for a change."

"Nah," Boone said, and the other guys nodded. "Ella is Ella. She doesn't need special treatment. In fact, she hates it. Right?"

Ella opened her mouth then closed it again. There was a downside to having proven her mettle to the guys for all those years, and this was it. They truly saw her as one of them. Hell, they probably thought she peed standing up. And it would never, ever enter their heads that she could fall head over heels in love.

Jesus. She was so screwed.

"I'm fine anywhere," Jake offered.

Mighty fine, her fox said dreamily.

"You'll both stay at the plantation house," Kai said in a *that's that* tone. With Silas away, Kai was the ranking shifter at Koa Point. "It makes the most sense. Plus, we might need the guesthouse for that guy Silas was trying to negotiate with."

Ella frowned. That guy, she'd heard, was a lion shifter. Or was it a tiger? She could never remember which. Some high-up in the feline shifter world that Silas was eager to establish a peace pact with after recent tensions involving a rogue lion-vampire mix. She wished Silas were around to clarify, but he and Cassandra were in New York, trying to track down the last of the Spirit Stones.

"Nothing's a problem for Jake," Boone said, smacking him on the back. "We can count on him."

"Happy to help," Jake said in that steady, boy-next-door way.

Ella was tempted to blurt out the whole sad story. *I love Jake. I need Jake. But if we get too close, I won't be able to resist him like before. He's my destined mate.*

But she couldn't say any such thing. The guys would probably joke that she only loved her M16. The women would wink and tell her to enjoy the night. Jake, meanwhile, didn't know about shifters or destined mates. Hell, if she told him, he'd probably run for the hills. Or worse, he'd declare himself tough enough to handle anything and get himself killed for honor's sake.

So she kept her lips glued together and caved in. "Fine."

But it wasn't fine, and she knew it. Somehow, she had to find a way out of this mess.

Chapter Three

Jake pounded down the shoulder of the highway on what had become his regular evening run, not so much taking in the sunset as mulling over the past week — his first on Maui. The work was good. The people were good. But Ella — Christ, she still made his body rage with need.

Hence the running, which he hoped would sweat the desire out of him. Not that it worked. So maybe he had to rethink the *get her off my mind* plan and try something else — like *get her out of my system by giving in to temptation* instead. Surely, he and she would burn through each other within a couple of days. Chemistry that intense wouldn't last forever, right?

A low, grumbly voice cackled in the back of his mind. *Wanna bet?*

A red Ferrari zipped by in the oncoming lane, and the driver waved out the open top. "Hey, man. Slow down."

Jake shook his head. Only Boone would break the speed limit in his sports car and yell at a runner to slow down.

"Maybe you—" Jake started to retort, but he broke off when a police vehicle appeared in hot pursuit. The lights were flashing, and Officer Dawn Meli — Hunter's partner — waved to Jake as she flew by.

Jake grinned. "Never mind." From what he'd heard, Dawn ticketed Boone practically every week.

He ran on, and within three steps, his mind was back on Ella. She might be one of the guys to the rest of her unit, but to him... She was everything he'd ever want in an army buddy combined with everything he'd ever dreamed of in a woman, all wrapped into one.

So, obviously, his interest in Ella hadn't faded — not over the past year and a half, when he hadn't touched another woman, though not for lack of offers — and certainly not over the past week. What he couldn't figure out was Ella's side of things. Did her mind blur every time they came close, sending zaps of sensual energy through her body until it was hard to see straight? Did the thrill — the feeling of an addiction waiting to happen — tempt her the way it tempted him?

A truck rattled by in the southbound lane, and Jake picked up the pace for the last two miles of his run, pushing his body hard. Usually, he could tune out everything when he got in the zone, but Ella never left his mind.

For the past week, she'd avoided him — unusual behavior for a woman more likely to chew out a man's ass if she caught him checking out *her* ass or slacking on the job. When he and she did occupy the same time and space, Ella was cool, distant, and strictly professional.

So maybe she wasn't interested in him, after all.

But from time to time, he'd catch her eyes flash before they flicked away, and he knew. Eyes didn't lie, as his mother used to say whenever she caught him or one of his brothers up to no good. And Ella's eyes — while near-impossible to catch hold of these days — sparkled every time he managed to pin them down. So, yeah. Ella felt what he did and as intensely.

So why did she open her mouth as if to say *Jake, I need to tell you something* but then snap it shut and hurry away? Why did she look up from petting Keiki to share a wide, easy grin — then go grim as if she'd just remembered something terrible about him?

"Whoa! Watch it." He darted toward the edge of the road as a car zipped by, too close for comfort. He turned for a second look as it sped on, weaving back to the center of its lane before disappearing around a bend.

Another tourist, he figured, too busy checking out the sunset to watch the road.

He pounded onward, pumping his arms, assuring himself that the couple of injuries he'd sustained over the years hadn't left a permanent mark. He thought about the night ahead too, and his new job.

So far, it was working out well — at least, as far as work went. Kai had assigned him and Ella the night shift from 22:00 to 06:00, with him covering the plantation perimeter, while Ella patrolled the outer boundaries of the main estate. So, really, it was an ordinary patrol schedule like he'd worked countless times before. And, hell. It sure beat the Middle East, even if he did have to deal with the temptation of Ella every day. In some ways, there was a reassuring familiarity to the whole routine — striding soundlessly through the shadows and underbrush, keeping his senses piqued. Stopping to listen for sounds that didn't fit. Pacing along the mile-long perimeter of the plantation, making sure everyone was safe and secure.

The unusual part of the job was the fact that the guys of Koa Point threw in their own, overlapping patrols on a schedule they refused to share. That and the fact that the others studied every detail as if they were in a war zone and the slightest oversight could mean life or death. They insisted on checking out the smallest irregularity, which is why Jake had pointed out the footprints he'd found the first night.

"How about these wolf tracks?" he'd asked.

Hunter had dismissed those after one quick look. "Just a big dog. See that nick between the toes? He's around here all the time. Nothing to worry about."

Jake squinted at the tracks. He would have sworn that was a wolf. There were two other sets of canine prints Hunter also okayed. "But any other dog prints, you tell us about right away. Roger?"

Jake had nodded. "Roger."

A little weird, but what the heck. If Hunter wasn't worried about big dogs, neither was he. Other than the pair of teens looking for a place to make out he'd sent packing the first night — sorry, kids — there'd been nothing out of the ordinary. In many ways, it was a comfortable echo of his structured military life, and that suited him fine. Hypervigilance was a plus in this job, so that fish-out-of-water feeling didn't strike him as much as it had over the previous few weeks.

"Everything fine? How are you settling in?" Tessa had asked. "Anything we can get you?"

"Got everything I want," he'd replied. If he didn't count Ella, he really did have everything. But he was burning with the desire to talk to Ella — even just once — and figure things out.

Okay, and maybe burning with some other desires, too.

Ella aside, it was one of the more low-key assignments he'd ever had. Whatever downtime Jake didn't spend catching up on sleep or running, he devoted to practicing sitting out in the open without constantly surveying the bushes for enemy outposts. He'd found a pile of dusty old puzzles in a corner of his room and started piecing them together out there on the porch. Puzzles kept his mind busy without letting it get *too* busy, so it was therapeutic in a way. The design didn't matter so much — just the satisfaction of all those pieces snapping neatly into place, forming a whole instead of a mess of parts. Which probably said a lot about his state of mind, though he decided not to dwell on that.

He checked his watch as he leaned into the last turn of his run, pushing harder. Totally in the zone now, hammering away, feeling good—

His smooth step faltered as he twisted to look over his shoulder at whatever his sixth sense alerted him to.

"What the..." he muttered as a car sped into view.

He'd been running in the shoulder of the oncoming lane to keep an eye on each car as it sped by, while the cars coming from behind him were all the way over on the other side. But that white sedan didn't stay on its side. It accelerated across the road and came right at him.

"Hey!" he yelled, waving the driver away. "Watch it!" But the car kept coming as if intent on flattening him.

Then he realized that car was definitely coming for him. Engine roaring, tires spinning, front grate grinning at him like a hungry shark. He waited one more second then dove for the side of the road.

Beeeeep! The car whooshed past an inch from his heels.

Jake crashed through a roadside bush and rolled when as he hit the ground. A split second later, he scrambled to his feet and spun to face the road.

"What the hell?" he muttered as the car raced out of sight. He listened for a full minute, barely moving except for his heaving chest. Was that idiot coming back? All he'd really caught was the silhouette of a tall man with long, wispy hair. Was nearly killing someone that guy's idea of a prank?

Slowly, Jake leaned over and dusted off his legs. He was scraped all over and bleeding from a couple of scratches, though it was nothing a shower couldn't fix. But the sight of the car hurtling right toward him — that stuck in his mind.

"Asshole."

He edged back to the road and started running again, watching and listening in case the idiot made another pass. He was fairly sure it was the same white sedan that had passed earlier — but then again, those rental cars all looked alike. Two minutes later, he stopped at the branch-off to the private road to Koa Point and the plantation grounds, watching the road like a hawk. Finally, he jogged down the lane to cool off. His heart still hammered in his chest, though, and his mind spun wildly. Why would anyone do such a thing?

He slowed to a walk when he approached the house, still absorbed in what had just happened. But out of nowhere, Ella's voice stopped him in his tracks. All business, all military.

"McBride. Meeting tonight at 20:00."

He looked up and found her standing on the porch of the once-grand plantation house. The homestead spread twice as wide as the big house on his family's ranch, its length accentuated by a long, sprawling porch that took in a huge, seemingly endless ocean view. But the roof sagged in places, the floorboards were rotting, and most of the rooms were unused.

He nodded. "20:00 tonight. Any idea what it's about?"

When Ella shook her head, her ponytail waved around, and the last rays of sunlight glinted in it. God, he loved that. A little hint of her feminine side in spite of everything she did to look tough.

"Silas and Cassandra are coming home. Everyone always gets together for that."

That sounded like good news, but Ella's mood was somber and her shoulders tense, giving him the distinct impression something had come up — something more than just the return of their commander and his fiancée.

Over the past days, it had gradually dawned on him how concerned everyone was about whatever business Silas was taking care of in New York. Like it wasn't just business but something much more important than that. Something connected to the enemies they'd hinted at, perhaps, and the need to watch over the estate constantly. He'd come across Boone and Kai discussing Silas's search — or had they said research? Either way, they'd shut up when he came near, and it hadn't been his place to ask. But something was definitely up.

"Whoa." Ella did a double take, staring at his scratched legs. "What happened?"

"Nothing," he muttered, heading for his end of the house. Ella had assigned him the north wing when he'd moved in — as far from her quarters in the south wing as possible.

But now, she pulled him into the light and studied his bloodied elbows. "Nothing happened?"

"It's all superficial."

She crooked an eyebrow at him. "And it happened when. . . ?"

When some maniac tried to run me off the road flew to the tip of his tongue, but all he said was, "I lost my footing somewhere along the line."

She snorted. "Right. Jake McBride, losing his footing. Being clumsy. Is that what they gave you the Distinguished Service Cross for?"

He couldn't help but swell with pride. So Ella knew he'd earned one. Not that he'd ever acted in the hope of collecting medals — just to get his unit to safety and to get a job done.

"Guess I wasn't paying attention."

She snorted even louder. "Right. Sure." Then she pointed to one of the chairs on the porch. "Let me have a look."

"It's nothing. Just a few scratches."

"Sit," she ordered, giving him a little shove. "And tell me what really happened."

He plonked down in the creaky porch chair, protesting the whole time. She kneeled, grabbed one of the napkins left under a rock on the porch table — one of Tessa's attempts at civilizing the place — and dabbed at his bloody shin.

"I was running... Ow." He grimaced as she plucked a thorn from an open cut. Of course, it was kind of nice to have her fuss over him. Really nice, if he were honest.

"Don't be a baby. Now sit still."

He did sit still, mainly because she was so close. The light of the setting sun glinted off her hair, giving it that coppery sheen he sometimes glimpsed. He inhaled deeply, savoring her faint, floral scent. A scent that reminded him of untouched plains and mile-high mountains. Home, in a word.

Ella put a hand on his knee and rose a little higher, checking his thigh. Blood rushed through his veins, and the minor aches and pains faded away, replaced by a warm, sweet heat.

And... damn. It was happening again. That invisible force, that black hole that sucked him in whenever he got too close to Ella.

"So tell me..." Ella looked up and trailed off, catching the way he looked at her. And hell, the pink in her cheeks gave her away too. Her lips shone, and her eyes seemed to glow. Which had to be a trick of the light, but wow. She leaned closer, and Jake heated in anticipation. A kiss. What he wouldn't give for a kiss.

They both leaned closer, focused entirely on each other's lips—

"Damn it," Ella muttered, jerking to her feet.

Jake blinked a couple of times then stood without thinking, making the chair screech. "Ella. Wait."

But she didn't wait. She took two shaky steps away, muttering to herself.

"What is it?" he demanded, suddenly tired of messing around.

She looked at her feet. "There's that meeting Kai called at eight."

He shook his head. "What is it with us, I mean?"

A tic set in on her right cheek, and she scowled at a rotting floorboard. "What us?"

He took a step closer. "Us, *us*. That night. That one time we—"

Her cheeks went red, and her eyes darted all over the place — except toward him. "That didn't happen."

She might as well have stuck that big Bowie knife of hers in his gut and twisted a few times. "It didn't happen?"

Ella whirled to walk away, but he followed, feeling his face heat.

"It didn't happen?" His voice rose, but he couldn't help it, and he grabbed her hand to stop her. "That night was one of the only good things that happened in that whole mess of a war. And you're saying it didn't happen?"

Ella's eyes flashed as she backed toward the wall. "We said we'd keep it to just that one night."

He followed, not wanting to cage her in but determined not to let her run this time.

"I've tried, Ella. You've tried. But it's still there." He waved in the few inches between their bodies. "It's like something else is driving this, and I have no idea what it is."

Her eyes flashed with emotions he couldn't read, and a single word fell from her lips. "Destiny."

It sounded strangely ominous, matching Ella's stricken expression.

"Whatever it is, I'm sick of fighting it. Don't you think we ought to give *us* another chance?"

The flash in her eyes said *yes*, so he kept pressing forward with careful steps until Ella was nearly backed against the outer wall of the house, leaving her enough space to slide away if she insisted. But she didn't. She just glared at him. Or rather, glared *through* him as if to blame someone — or something — else for what had happened back then.

"Say something. Say anything," he growled. "Just don't say it never happened. Say you regret it if you have to—"

She shook her head immediately. "I never said I regretted it."

He gulped, staring at her. "Then what? What is it that's holding us back?"

Ella grimaced. "Things you can't understand."

"So, explain."

She shook her head again. "I can't."

Jake tilted his head, studying her. He'd never seen Ella look so stuck or helpless. Ella didn't do helpless. She didn't know the meaning of *I can't.*

He leaned closer until his lips were an inch away from hers. Less than an inch, maybe.

"Please tell me, Ella," he whispered. "Tell me you're not interested. Tell me you don't want me."

"I do want you."

It was ridiculous what a few words could do to a man's heart, no matter how hard he tried to keep it locked away.

"Then why do you keep pushing me away?"

She didn't reply, but she didn't move away. In fact, her hands clutched at his shirt, keeping him close. He nestled closer, sliding his arms over her shoulders, drawn by that body-to-body gravity that set in every time they got too close.

Ella moved her lips, but no sound came out. Or maybe he'd gone deaf, because all he heard was a roaring in his ears. Her arms slid around his waist, and her eyes shone with an inner battle he felt too.

Kiss her, a little voice urged from the back of his mind.

God, he wanted to. Bad.

The roaring grew louder, like a tsunami rushing toward the shore.

She wants it too, the voice insisted. *Bad.*

Ella eased back, pulling him with her until he had her pinned against the wall. Her move, not his, like she wanted to surrender but didn't know how.

His pulse revved up into overdrive, and his nerves reported everything at once, drowning him in sensations. The tight grip of her arms. The heat of her chest. The desert rose scent of her hair. The burning need to hold her, countered by the fear of getting in way over his head.

Gradually, every input disappeared except one, and all he felt was the soft pillow of her lips as she kissed him. The second she did, the whirlwind in his soul vanished, leaving him with a sense of peace.

Ella threaded her fingers through his hair and guided him to exactly the angle she sought, moving her lips over his. Kissing. Touching. Barely breathing, like him.

He caught her lower lip between his and pressed it gently before letting her taste him.

It felt so good. Like coming home should have felt after all that time away. Like getting everything he ever wanted all delivered on the same day. He pulled her closer and kissed harder, cursing his own weakness for her even as he hungered for more. No woman had ever done to him what Ella could do with a single kiss.

"We shouldn't do this," she mumbled without pulling away.

"I agree," he said between kisses, then dove in for another. His hands traced her sides as her body surged toward his.

But a minute later, Ella pulled away, chest heaving, holding him close. She rested her forehead on his chest and spoke into his shirt.

"We can't let this happen," Ella whispered, though she made no move to let go.

Jake gave up asking why. He just held on to her.

"Jake..."

He looked at her, wishing he knew what he wanted to say. *Stop resisting this, Ella?* Or should he say, *You're right. We can't let this happen?* Whatever power was at work between them — destiny? Raw desire? — was beyond addictive, and he hated how it had overrode all his self-control.

"Maybe we should—" Ella started.

But damn it, he'd left his phone atop the puzzle on the porch table earlier, and its ring cut through the air.

You want to answer that? Ella's look asked.

Jake shook his head. Not really, not now. "Listen—"

But the phone rang with urgency, and Ella nudged him. "Maybe you should get that."

Jake reached for the damn thing, eyeing the surrounding bushes for a boulder he could smash it against. Who the hell was calling him now?

"Damn it, Hoover," he barked, picking up after a glance at the number. It was always good to touch base with his army buddies, but Hoover was constantly calling to share outrageous theories or to rant against civilian life. "Not now—"

"Manny is dead." The voice that came across the line was rattled and spooked.

Jake stopped cold. "What?"

Ella looked up.

He turned away as the blood drained from his face. "Fuck, man. What happened?"

"Single shot to the head," Hoover said. "Forty-five caliber."

Jake stared into the distance, tempted to shove the table sideways and roar. Another good friend dead. Worse — that made Manny the third member of their unit to have died in the past few weeks. How could that be possible? They'd served together for years and survived too many tight situations to count — and now this.

He clutched the phone so hard, he was surprised it didn't shatter in his hand. "Why? Who?"

"The cops are calling it a robbery gone wrong, but I'm not buying that shit," Hoover half whispered, half shouted over the crackly connection. "I'm telling you, man. Someone is taking us out, one by one."

Jake froze, picturing the white sedan roaring toward him. Maybe that hadn't been a prank or a moment of inattention. Maybe it had been the real thing. And, shit — if Hoover wasn't imagining things, then that could be connected to Junger's climbing accident and Chalsmith's car wreck. Or was Hoover making him paranoid, too?

"Think about it, man," Hoover went on in his hoarse, *conspiracy theory* tone. "That patrol that went down. The ambush last June."

Jake's stomach lurched as it always did when he thought of that awful day. But what did that ambush have to do with anything?

Boom! He'd never forget the force or the sound of that explosion. Six men had been lost that day.

It should have been us, man, Hoover had said in the aftermath.

Jake hadn't been able to do anything but stare at his feet, because Hoover was right. Their vehicle had switched places with another in the convoy at the last minute, so it ought to have been them who'd been blown to bits.

Truthfully, I'm happy to be alive, Manny had said.

That somber evening had led to the discussion that put each man on a new course. Every member of the unit vowed to make the most of their second chance when their tour of duty was up. Junger was determined to climb Denali. Manny had opened an auto body shop with his dad. Chalsmith had been negotiating with his ex for more time with his kids, and Jake...

Jake had made up some shit about visiting all fifty states, though, really, he'd been secretly fighting the urge to find Ella and see if what they had was more than a one-night thing.

Destiny, she'd whispered.

Was there really such a thing?

"I'm telling you, man. Someone is after us," Hoover said.

Jake gripped the porch railing. Could it be true?

Ella touched his shoulder and mouthed, *Everything okay?*

He pursed his lips as images of Manny flooded his mind. He saw Manny laughing wildly, making another joke. Manny reading and rereading letters from back home. Jake dropped his chin to his chest and closed his eyes. Nothing was okay. Manny had been a good guy. A really good guy.

Ella put her hand on his shoulder. A second later, he put his hand over hers, and somehow, that helped. Two against all the crap in the world were definitely better than one.

"One of us is next, man," Hoover hissed. "And I swear, it ain't gonna be me."

Jake looked down at his scraped-up legs and scowled into the phone. "You want it to be me?"

"Sorry, man," Hoover backtracked. "That came out wrong. I don't want it to be you or me. I want to figure out who the bastard is, but it will take a while to track things down. If it's that asshole LeBonn like I think it is..."

Jake's mouth twisted into a grimace. He had no clue who LeBonn might be, but he knew Hoover all too well. A great guy at heart, but like a Doberman who never got walked, Hoover was overexcitable and quick to bark. Borderline paranoid maniac. How seriously should his words be taken?

He heard the screech of tires, the deafening horn as he replayed the memory of the white sedan racing toward him.

Ella squeezed his shoulder, and a little bit of his uneasiness crumbled away.

"We'll talk soon," Hoover said.

Jake nodded. At that moment, it didn't matter how Manny had died, only that another friend was gone. He needed time to digest the news before figuring out whether to follow Hoover into another crazy crusade — or to talk some sense into the man. "We'll talk soon. Take care, man."

"Yeah. You too."

Jake dropped the phone onto the puzzle and stared at it. Would someone else be dead the next time Hoover called? Who would want to wipe out an entire unit that hadn't done anything wrong?

A car beeped on the distant highway, and his head jerked up.

Ella's eyes followed his. "It's that blind turn. Lots of drivers underestimate it."

Jake frowned. Was it possible to underestimate it so badly as to zip across two lanes and nearly mow down a runner on the opposite side?

The hand he ran through his hair came out damp with sweat. Manny was dead. Hoover was paranoid. And he was a mess. Too flighty. Too on edge. Ready to believe Hoover's crazy ideas. Maybe he ought to keep away from Ella, who could do a lot better than a guy like him.

"You okay?" she whispered, running her arm over his shoulders.

"Fine." He cleared his throat and made a show of checking his watch. "Nearly time for that meeting. We'd better get moving."

"Jake," Ella whispered. Now she was the one holding on, and he was the one pulling away.

But it was better that way, and he knew it, so he strode down the porch toward his end of the big, empty house, determined not to look back.

Chapter Four

Ella forced herself to breathe evenly as she followed Jake down the winding path to Koa Point. No asking questions, no touching his arm, no words of comfort, even though it was obvious he needed them. Even after a shower and time to cool off, Jake was as shut off as... as...

As you've been to him? her fox grumbled.

Damn. The truth hurt. Make that, burned. If she could take it all back...

So take it back. Say something, her fox said.

What was she supposed to say? *I've been horrible to you because you're my mate, and I don't want you to die as miserably as my mother's mate did?*

Poor Brian. Poor Jake. Ella kicked a fallen branch aside. It killed her to see Jake so tense. So bottled up. So cold. But somehow, she had to stay strong and resist the call of her mate.

No! No! No! He needs us, and we need him, her fox whimpered. *Say something!*

"You okay?" she asked quietly.

"Fine," Jake grunted.

If he used *fine* the way she did... then, shit. The man must really be hurting inside. Of course he was, if a friend had just died. She'd gathered that much. But her chance to say something had passed because they were nearly in earshot of the others.

A long line of tiki torches led to the meeting house on Koa Point — more torches than most nights, even, perhaps as a nod to Silas, the alpha of Koa Point. He stood in the middle of a huddle of friends, not the biggest or burliest of the group, but with an unmistakable undercurrent of dragon power that

33

made the toughest of men step back. Jake, though, stepped right up to Silas, not intimidated in the least.

He'd make a great shifter, Ella's fox sighed.

"Ella. Jake. So good to have you here," Silas said as they shook hands.

"Good to be here," Jake replied.

Ella stared at the sight of Silas smiling — actually smiling. She'd been so focused on Jake, she hadn't noticed how happy Silas looked. Unabashedly, joyously happy. Almost relaxed, if a dragon could be called that.

"This is Cassandra, my m— Er, fiancée," Silas said.

Ella jabbed an elbow into Silas's ribs — alpha or no alpha, he couldn't afford to slip up. It had been bad enough to have Boone nearly blurting the word *mate* over the past week. Humans had no idea what that meant, and she sure wasn't going to explain to Jake.

But Silas barely noticed. He and Cassandra grinned at each other like a couple of love-struck teens, and Ella couldn't help marveling at the fact that yet another member of her unit had fallen deeply in love.

"Thanks so much for coming, Jake," Cassandra said.

"Did you have a good trip?" he asked, polite as ever.

Did you find the keystone? Boone asked Cassandra.

Ella nearly shushed him, but then she remembered only shifters could hear each other's thoughts. Damn it, Jake fit in so perfectly among the group, she kept forgetting he was human.

So, forget, her fox tried.

She couldn't afford to forget. Ever.

No Spirit Stone, Cassandra sighed. But that didn't seem to bother her much because a moment later, another knowing smile passed between the lovebirds. "It was a great trip." Then Cassandra's smile wavered. "Except we've come across one hitch in our plans."

Silas nodded wearily as everyone leaned in. For a long minute, the only sound was that of crickets chirping in the night.

"You're not getting married?" Boone, the jokester, asked, breaking the tension.

"Ha. Try stopping us," Cassandra laughed.

Silas kissed her hand, making Ella blink in disbelief. Wow. The mighty commander, showing emotion — in public?

Ella glanced around, frowning to discover everyone seemed to be wearing the same happily-ever-after look — except her, of course. "So what's the problem?"

Jake nodded, keeping his focus on Silas. Tuned in, as ever, to his job. The man was a born protector. A team player. A soldier, through and through.

If only he were a shifter too.

"We wanted to keep things small. A little ceremony just for us, here at Koa Point," Silas explained. "But unfortunately, word of our engagement has gotten out, and the press started hounding us."

Cassandra's lips curled in a wry grin. "The public can't get enough of Silas. Must be his social graces."

Everyone laughed — even Silas. "It has more to do with my inheritance, I'm afraid."

"Don't tell me you're doing a big celebrity wedding. We've had enough of those," Kai said, making everyone chuckle or groan.

"No way," Cassandra said quickly. "We want a small, private wedding. But we figure it's better to give the press something rather than letting them spin lies. So we've decided on a big reception at the Kapa'akea Resort a day before a quiet wedding here on the estate. That way, we call the shots instead of having the press snoop around."

Jake nodded thoughtfully. "Is that the big resort off the main road?"

Ella nodded. "The fancy place with the polo grounds."

"The penthouse suite is pretty nice." Boone grinned, looking at Nina.

Hunter rubbed his beard. "What about security?"

"Yeah. What about Moira?" Boone asked.

Ella scowled, as did everyone else. Even Jake, who didn't know Moira, caught on to the downturn in everyone's mood.

His brow knotted, and he looked grim. Ella wished she could send her thoughts into his mind with the details. *Moira is Silas's vengeful ex. One of the nastiest dragons of them all.*

But, hell. How could she even begin to explain the details of all that? Jake's jaw would drop at *dragon*, and he would never understand the archaic dynamics of the shifter world.

Cassandra gripped Silas's hand tightly, and the lines that had appeared on his brow eased.

"I don't think Moira will enter the equation, but you never know. She's tried underhanded moves before."

"Security at Kapa'akea should be straightforward, right?" Ella asked.

Everyone pulled a long face.

"An intruder managed to get in before. It could happen again," Kai said. "The question is how to prevent it this time."

"Double the security?" Nina suggested.

Silas shook his head. "That Vanderpelt wedding had all the security in the world, yet it didn't prevent that last-minute surprise."

"Are you worried about an inside job?" Tessa asked.

"I want *not* to be worried about an inside job," Silas said. "Which is why we came up with a special plan."

Ella did a double take when Silas's gaze landed solidly on her before continuing to Jake, who looked just as uncomfortable as she felt. Did they have something to do with that plan?

Jake didn't ask, though. He couldn't — not of a ranking officer. Even Ella hesitated. It didn't matter that they were all out of the service these days. Rank was rank, and beyond that, each of them owed Silas their lives — several times over, in fact.

"It's a big favor to ask," Silas said, looking between them. "But I think it's the only way."

Jake nodded the way Ella remembered him doing before setting off on one of the joint missions their units had carried out. Whatever Silas asked, Jake would do. Rappelling in from a chopper? No problem. Going solo behind enemy lines to create a distraction, even if it meant risking his life? Jake would be willing to do that too.

"We need an inside man," Kai said.

Ella blinked. *Inside man* suggested something like mingling with a crowd at that fancy resort, and there were two problems with that. One, Jake didn't seem too comfortable with crowds these days. Two, he was more of a jeans and boots guy, and surely, that wouldn't work at the ritzy club.

"Someone people around here wouldn't recognize," Silas explained.

Ella eyed him warily. "What exactly are you thinking of?"

"You and Jake..." Silas started.

Ella's fox wagged its tail.

"As insiders in the resort..." Silas went on.

Ella had no idea what Silas had in mind, but whatever it was, she didn't like it. "What, like catering staff or something?"

Silas grinned. "No, much easier than that. You'll pose as guests."

Ella crossed her arms and raised an eyebrow, not amused. "Guests? Like who, your cousins?"

Silas's smile stretched. "No. As far as the public is concerned, your stay will have nothing to do with our reception."

"Then why would we be there?"

Jake, she sensed, had the same bad feeling about this, but he still gave Silas a firm, *Yes, sir* nod. Until Kai filled in the rest, that is.

"As honeymooners, of course. Mr. and Mrs. Jacob McBride," Kai announced, looking awfully pleased with himself.

"Mr. and Mrs. *What*?" Ella screeched.

"Just think." Boone waggled his eyebrows. "Room service. Silk sheets. King-size bed."

Jake looked stunned. Ella couldn't believe her ears. Didn't anyone know what that meant?

Apparently not, because Kai just went on like he had everything figured out.

"It's perfect. No one will associate you with the reception, and we can plant you there a couple of days ahead of time to keep an eye out for anything suspicious."

Kai wanted her to try to resist Jake for a couple of days? The past week had been torture, but pretending to be married would be hell.

My kind of hell, her fox murmured, happily lashing her tail.

"The trick is to stick as close to the truth as possible when you make up a story," Kai went on. "So, you met overseas and fell madly in love..."

Ella exchanged looks with Jake and gulped. No need for fabrications so far.

"...You ran into each other a few months after being discharged and decided life was too short not to get married..." Kai continued.

She frowned, but Jake nodded like that was exactly his plan.

"...And here you are, on your honeymoon." Kai finished.

Ella put up her hands in a signal to stop. "Who's going to believe we could afford that place?"

Silas grinned. "Let's just say you found a generous benefactor with a soft spot for war heroes."

Ella shifted from foot to foot, searching for an excuse to reject the whole crazy plan.

Damn it, she ended up bellowing into her friends' minds so everyone but Jake could hear. *I can't do that. Jake can't do that. It's too much.*

Come on, Ella, Boone said, tilting his head toward Jake. *You know you like him. How hard can it be?*

I do not like him! What would give you such a stupid idea?

The guys exchanged knowing looks, and Hunter gave an apologetic bear shrug. *You talk in your sleep. I mean... now and then, what with shared barracks and all. Well, just a few times.*

Lots of times, Boone corrected. *And it's always about Jake.*

Her cheeks heated. *Don't you dare try to set us up.*

Kai grinned. *Why not? You two would be good together.*

Right. A shifter and a human. I could kill him with the mating bite.

Everyone froze, staring at her. *Who said anything about mating?* Kai asked.

Ella froze. Jesus, what had she just said? She looked at Jake, whose eyes darted around, clearly wondering what was going on.

"Listen," Jake said, breaking into the awkward silence that had stretched on too long. "I'm happy to help, but maybe we can think of a better plan."

"Maybe we should," Tessa said, coming to the rescue again.

Ella ought to have been relieved, but all she felt was a sinking sense of defeat. Of a dream nearly coming true, only to slip away.

Well, maybe... her fox started, not ready to give up.

Maybe, what?

Ella frowned as everyone waited for her. She'd come to Maui to help her friends, so it didn't feel right to say no. The idea of extra eyes inside the resort did make a lot of sense, and who would suspect a couple of honeymooners? There was Jake to consider too. A man like him needed a challenge, a mission. A team to contribute to and a regular diet of impossible odds to overcome. He needed this assignment to find his footing again.

Our mate needs us to help him, her fox said.

So maybe if she said yes to this crazy gig...

Yes! Yes! her fox cheered.

...and found a way to let him down gently or make him see all her inner faults...

No! No!

...then she could help Jake get his head to where it needed to be to settle into civilian life again.

She pursed her lips. Was that crazy, or could she possibly resist Jake long enough to help him?

Worst case, she would explain about shifters. The idea of her turning into a fox with whiskers, four legs, and a tail would turn Jake off, for sure. If it didn't — well, she'd have to figure something else out. Like the truth.

She gulped, wondering how that might go.

I want you, Jake, but mating could kill you, so you're really better off with someone else.

Ella took a deep breath, ordering herself to abort the mission before it started. But Silas was looking at her, tapping his foot. Jake's eyes were fixed on her like a man awaiting judgment in a higher court.

She rehearsed her response once or twice in her head. *No. Absolutely not. I'm out of here.*

But all she managed to say was, "Not one of your better plans, Kai."

Jake let out a slow breath and leaned forward slightly.

"Aw, come on. If anyone can pull it off, you can." Kai grinned.

Ella wished he would consider what was at stake. But Silas's safety was at stake too, and Silas was part of her unit. A soldier didn't turn her back on her unit, no matter what.

She looked at Jake. "I'm not sure you know what you're getting into."

He shrugged, and his lips curled into a slight smile, making her knees go weak. "I'm in if you're in."

Every alarm in her brain was clanging desperately, though her inner fox just cooed and hummed.

She wavered for another second, searching for the strength to say no. But all that came out was a weak, "All right, then. I guess we're in."

Hopefully, those wouldn't become famous last words.

"Thank you so much," Cassandra gushed, hugging her tightly. "I know it's a lot to ask."

If only you knew, Ella nearly said.

"So, our next steps..." Kai mused.

Silas ticked off his fingers. "They'll need a marriage certificate."

Ella's head whipped around. "Whoa. How about forging one?"

Silas shook his head. "We want this to be ironclad. You can get divorced afterward."

"Divorced?" Jake's grin vanished.

40

"You can get married in Oahu — there are fewer people who might recognize Ella there — and fly over to Maui for your honeymoon. All very spontaneous."

"Oh, it's spontaneous, all right," Ella muttered.

Tessa looked skeptical. "I think it could work, but they'll need a little coaching for anyone to believe they're really honeymooners."

Boone laughed. "Ella will need a *lot* of coaching. Somehow, I can't picture her in a white dress."

"Funny, I can picture you in one," she shot back. But, damn. Boone was right. She hadn't worn a dress since she was about ten.

Boone put his hands on the sarong wrapped around his waist and winked. "Real men have no problems with skirts."

"Then maybe you should marry Jake," she tried. The second she said it, her fox growled.

No one's getting Jake but me.

Ella rolled her eyes. The beast was taking the whole absurd idea too literally.

"He is cute," Boone joked, putting an arm around Nina. "But sadly, I'm not the eligible bachelor I once was. So we'd better stick to you two as the happy couple."

And who knows, he added, waggling his eyebrows at her. *You might even have some fun.*

"They definitely need coaching," Nina said, letting her eyes flit between Ella and Jake. "You know, to warm up to each other a little."

Ella crossed her arms over her chest. She was steel-hard, cool, and collected, and she had to stay that way, because the only other gear she had around Jake was panting like a fox in heat.

Kai flapped a hand. "So show us *happy couple* already."

Ella scowled and shuffled a step closer to Jake, who slid a stiff arm across her shoulders. She wiggled and frowned, pretending she hated every minute of it. But a warm, happy glow filled her veins, and she found herself pressing against his side. Damn, that felt good. Like light filling her soul, chasing the loneliness away. Like hope and goodness and—

She caught herself there. Christ, she really had to watch out.

Tessa looked skeptical. "They need a lot of coaching."

"Hey," Ella protested.

"Different clothes would help," Cassandra said, tapping her lips.

Ella looked down at herself. Okay, so she was wearing her usual fatigue pants and a green tank top. Wisps of hair had escaped her ponytail, and her skin was layered with dust from a long day. In other words, business as usual. Nothing wrong with that. And Jake looked fine too...

Really fine, her fox hummed.

...in that olive T-shirt that stretched across his chest just so. His brown hair was an inch longer than he'd had it in the army, and that suited him. The bulge of his bicep rested comfortably over her shoulder, and his hip warmed her side.

"You need some serious coaching." Dawn sighed.

"Hey," Ella and Jake both protested at the same time.

Kai waved their protest away. "We'll figure it out. You two just play your parts."

Dawn broke into a smile. "Don't worry. I know just the person you need. As a coach, I mean."

Ella bit her lip. Oh, she would worry, all right.

Chapter Five

The perfect person for the job, as Ella discovered, was Lily, a bubbly local and friend of Dawn's.

"Oh, isn't this just wonderful?" Lily gushed early the next morning. Her *mu'umu'u* flapped wildly as they walked toward Kai's helicopter in a crouch. "All so exciting."

Ella kept her lips sealed. Although she'd helicoptered or rappelled into dozens of missions in the past, this seemed like the most dangerous one of all.

But, *zoom* — it all happened in what seemed like the blink of an eye. The flight to Oahu. The taxi ride to city hall. She nearly balked at the threshold, but Jake nudged her over with a grin she couldn't read. Did he love the idea of a sham marriage? Hate it? Something in between?

"Do you, Ella Louise Kitt, take Jacob Michael McBride. . . " the official said in a totally flat tone.

Ella blinked a few times. How on earth had she ever agreed? *To have and to hold* was far, far too tempting a prospect when it came to the man with puppy dog eyes and full, all-too-kissable lips.

But Jake's hand was warm and comforting around hers, and when he kissed her, they both ended up hanging on a little too long.

"I now pronounce you man and wife."

"Holy shit," she blurted half an hour later, still reeling from it all. "I'm married."

Married to Jake. Her fox wagged its tail. *Don't worry. Everything will be all right.*

"Don't worry," Lily chirped, beaming.

43

Ella made a face. Nothing made her stress more than *Don't worry.*

"I have it all planned out," Lily said. "You and I will go shopping..."

I hate shopping, Ella grunted at Kai, who just grinned.

"...while Kai and Jake do their thing," Lily finished.

Ella had no idea what that *thing* was, but the men went off in one direction, while she and Lily went in another.

"Oh, this is going to be so fun," Lily squeaked, dragging her toward a store on Honolulu's Kalakaua Avenue with Silas's platinum card in her hand.

Ella made a face. Fun in one of Oahu's priciest boutiques? It might have been fun if she were one of those pretty-in-pink types, but that just wasn't her. She liked practical clothes. Earth tones. Pockets to stow combat gear and other essentials, like her Swiss Army knife. Granola bars. Grenades.

"Ladies, we need help," Lily announced the second they entered the store.

Three saleswomen descended on Ella like locusts, and the torture began.

"No way. Never." She waved away the saleswoman brandishing a glittery strapless thing.

Lily waved the woman closer. "Oh, it's you."

Ella grimaced. That dress was so not her, it wasn't funny. The only thing worse was the matching underwear. She gaped at the price tag. "Why is it that the less fabric something is made of, the more it costs?"

"That's fashion," Lily sighed. "Anyway, I think the long-sleeved dress is better. You know, to cover the tattoos."

Ella looked at the patterns etched into her upper arms. One swirling pattern was a subtle tribute to her mother and Brian, reminding her to never, ever forget. The other she'd picked up when her entire unit had theirs done on a short R&R in Bangkok. "What's wrong with my tattoos?"

Lily turned to the saleswomen as if she hadn't heard. "Maybe something in green?"

The women scattered. When they reappeared, one carried green shoes that might have suited Dorothy for a trip to Oz.

Another held up a sleeveless number with a plunging neckline Ella could never pull off, and a third waved a tight silk dress with tiny knot buttons.

"Cassandra could get away with wearing that, but not me," Ella said, pointing at the dragon embroidered down one side of the fabric.

"Don't be silly. You have the perfect figure for that dress."

Ella had the perfect figure for charging across rocky landscapes or crawling under barbed wire, but definitely not for that dress. "I'd barely fill it out."

"Nonsense. Oh! Look at that." Lily's eyes widened at the next item — a pink chiffon jumper that almost made the green strapless number look acceptable. Then she checked her watch. "So many dresses, so little time. Ladies, we'll take them all."

"What?" Ella yelped.

Lily just waved a hand while the saleswomen rushed to pack what appeared to be half the store. "Add a few casual things too. Oh, and that adorable bikini."

"That adorable what?" Ella sputtered.

Lily smiled her *isn't this all so wonderful?* smile. "We'll pick them up in about an hour."

Ella eyed the back door. Running from a challenge had never been her style, but hell. She was in over her head with this one.

"Come, come," Lily clucked, grabbing her hand. "We have to get moving. We have to meet the men at the airport soon..."

Lily said *men* like they were some different, fascinating species, but Ella had spent her whole life in male-dominated domains. What was the big deal?

"We're nearly out of time, and we haven't even gotten your hair done yet."

Ella jerked a hand to her head. "What's wrong with my hair?"

Lily gave her a distinct, *Where do I begin?* look, but all she said was, "Trust me."

Ella gritted her teeth. *Trust me* was second in line to *Don't worry.*

Two hours later, Ella and Lily crammed into a taxi with a sinful number of bags — a minivan taxi, because a normal one would be too small — and headed to the airport.

"It would be so much easier for Kai to fly us back," Ella grumbled. Not that the helicopter stood a chance of lifting off with the weight of the new his-and-hers luggage Lily had picked out along with everything else. "Or to call off this whole honeymoon."

Lily clapped with glee. "See? You're internalizing it already. That's great."

Not great, Ella wanted to bark.

"Plus, it's part of your cover story," Lily added.

Ella had to give her that one. To anyone on Maui who cared to note such things, she and Jake would look like just another pair of honeymooners stepping off a commercial flight. When they arrived at the Kapa'akea Resort, everything would appear legit.

"Yoo-hoo! Kai," Lily hollered across the airport.

"Hi," Kai said, helping the driver unload the bags. When he turned and noticed Ella, he did a double take.

"Holy shit, Ella. Is that really you?"

Ella scowled and grunted. "Not sure any more."

"Now, now. Is that the way to talk to the happy bride?" Lily chided.

Kai stared, looking her up and down. "No. Yes. Sorry. I mean... Wow, Ella. You look so good."

She rolled her eyes. "And I punch really hard. Just remember that before you open your mouth again."

Kai turned slightly, keeping his groin out of kicking range. Her *hānai* brother knew her too well.

"Now all we need is the dashing groom," Lily said, looking around.

Ella made a face. Lily had missed her calling in life. She could have hosted a reality show called *Reluctant Brides* or *Spontaneous Wedding Bells.*

"He's on the way." Kai poked Ella in the upper arm. "Wow. It really is you."

"Watch it, Beaver Brain," she muttered, reverting to the nickname she and Hunter used to pester Kai with when they were kids.

"Oh, there he is," Lily chirped.

Ella turned around with a sigh. Fine. Time to pretend she was—

"Jake?" she squeaked. The moment she spotted him coming toward her, she froze, and every grouchy thought fled her mind.

Yu-um, her fox whistled, thumping its tail.

Maybe it wasn't Jake. Maybe he had a twin brother who modeled for fancy colognes or Armani suits. But then she spotted the tiny scar on his upper lip. Wow. It really was him. Regular old Jake always looked good in an All-American, G.I.-Joe way. But this Jake was drop-dead gorgeous. His sideburns had been trimmed back and given a sharp line that echoed the angles of his cheeks. And, wow. Either Kai had managed to get a suit tailored in record time, or Jake was one of those perfectly proportioned men who could slip into any garment and make it look like a second skin.

Perfect, her fox murmured.

The cut of his jacket showed off his tapered body, and the slacks hinted at the slabs of muscle underneath. His sky-blue eyes looked brighter than ever against the navy cloth, and he'd traded his boots for leather shoes that shone in the light.

Jake stopped and stared at her too. Ella wished for pockets to shove her hands into, but there weren't any in the airy, copper-colored sundress Lily had made her change into at the last shop. The hairdresser had insisted on shampooing her hair twice, blow-drying it to bits, and keeping it loose, so it waved every time she moved her head. That drove her crazy, but Jake didn't seem to mind.

"Ella," he murmured.

She couldn't move. She couldn't speak, because the only section of her brain that still operated was the part that didn't know about danger, limits, or regrets.

Lily nudged her. "Come along, now. Play the part. Honeymoon, remember?"

47

Ella's blood rushed as her mind flooded with thoughts of how nice it would be to spend a happy lifetime with Jake. To stop denying herself and revel in the purest, deepest form of love. The kind destiny sprinkled on a lucky few and gifted with joyous, fulfilling lives. She saw things she'd never allowed herself to picture before, like long, sunset walks with Jake — not on Maui, but back in Arizona, where red-tinted rocks flamed in the last hour of daylight. Better yet, a sunset run in fox form or cozy midnight hours gazing at the stars with Jake warming her side. The subtle turn of seasons and the absence of any pressing rush that allowed every precious minute to stretch into an hour.

Her lips moved. Her feet shuffled. And before she knew it, she was right in front of him. She tipped her chin up — way up, because being that close emphasized their height difference — and cupped his cheek.

"You look nice," he whispered, gazing into her eyes.

"So do you," she mumbled.

His arms slid around her waist like that was the most natural thing in the world to do, and they stood silently gaping at each other.

"Not bad for a start," Kai muttered from somewhere behind them.

Ella barely heard, because it wasn't an act. It was the real thing.

"Now, kiss," Lily hissed in *sotto voce* that half the airport could hear. "Kiss."

Ella should have stomped away and refused, but most of her brain had turned off, so. . .

She leaned closer, closed her eyes, and met Jake halfway for a kiss. The second their lips met, she clutched his shirt because, wow, what a kiss.

That kiss made breathing secondary and pushed away the outside world until she was in a tunnel of blindingly bright light, filled with honest, earthy flavors that went from *new* to her *absolute favorite* in an instant. It was the kind of kiss that filled her mind with a whirlwind of wild ideas, like hanging on to that marriage certificate forever and making this real.

But it wasn't real, and her eyelids fluttered, blinking back tears.

Jake stayed lost in the kiss a few seconds longer than she did, and when he opened his eyes, his chest rose with a deep breath.

Ella bit her lip. Whatever happened in the next few days, she vowed to never, ever hurt him. No more silent treatment like she'd tried over the past few days. No snippy comebacks, no single-syllable responses. She would give Jake all the warmth and respect he deserved, and somehow, she would make him understand how impossible the idea of being together was.

Her fox wailed inside. *I want to be together. Forever.*

She swallowed hard. *Forever* wasn't in the cards for her and Jake. But a week she never thought she'd get? She could pack a lifetime of love and living into that time. The only trick would be finding the strength to let him go at the end.

"Not bad," Kai chuckled.

Ella ignored her almost-big-brother and hugged Jake fiercely. She might not be able to explain her secret vow to him, but she could show him she cared. Jake seemed intent on the same thing, because he held her tightly, stroking her hair just as he'd done on that magical night they'd shared a long time ago.

"Time to check in," Kai said.

Slowly, gently, Ella eased away from Jake, trying to focus on her next steps.

Lily poked her arm. "Don't forget to keep holding hands."

Funny, Ella didn't need a reminder that time.

When Kai pushed the luggage cart and led them to a counter, Jake looked up in surprise.

"Business class?"

Kai grinned. "When Silas does something, he does it in style. Besides, we're treating this as a hardship post." His eyes twinkled. Had he caught on that that might not be the case?

Lily beamed at the airline agent. "They're honeymooners! Isn't that wonderful?"

"That is wonderful," the man behind the counter agreed, checking their IDs. "Mr. McBride and Mrs..." He frowned. "Ms. Kitt?"

"She's keeping her name," Jake growled in a distinct, *You got a problem with that?* tone.

He'd make a great shifter, her fox cooed as the agent shrank back.

Ella tightened her grip around Jake's hand. He had always accepted her as she was, letting her be herself. A prince of a man, and she was supposed to give him up? How?

She looked around the concourse. Businessmen bustled by, and couples walked hand in hand. A child ran from her mother into an older couple's arms, crying, "Grandma! Grandpa!" A group of fresh arrivals bustled toward their bus, eager to leave the humdrum of daily life behind and explore a new place.

Ella's chest rose and fell. Maybe that's what she and Jake needed — to let go of the past. To step away from the roles they had both grown accustomed to and to explore. Maybe even to reinvent themselves and find something other than *rock-hard soldier* inside.

"That will be gate fifty-six," the man at the counter said. "Have a nice flight."

Lily beamed her thanks. *"Mahalo."*

Kai and Lily walked them most of the way to the security check.

"You good to go?" Kai asked.

"Good to go." Jake nodded, waiting for Ella to nod before taking her hand.

"Roger," she said, trying to sound businesslike instead of breathy — and failing miserably. Was there anything *not* to love about Jake?

Kai grinned and waved toward the gate. "Well, then. Have fun, kids."

Chapter Six

Oh, we'll have fun, all right, Ella's fox murmured.

She took a deep breath. God, this was going to be torture.

The best kind of torture.

"Have a great honeymoon." Lily clucked over Ella and Jake and waved them off with a tear in her eye. Almost as if it was a real honeymoon, and Lily was the bride's mom.

Ella's eyes grew misty as she thought back to Georgia Mae, the kind owl shifter who had given her, Hunter, and Kai a stable, loving home after her mother died of grief. Over the years, Ella had often thought of Georgia Mae's generosity, but she had never really stopped to consider what Georgia Mae would feel as her charges grew up and hit major landmarks. Like this one – marriage. Even if it was a sham, it made Ella think. Would Georgia Mae approve of Jake and this whole crazy venture?

Ella wove her fingers between Jake's as they walked through security, finally on their own. In some ways, it was a lot like the military — even on a mission assigned by higher-ups, once a team struck out, the mission became their own. Other than a scribbled list of instructions Lily had given her – yes, instructions, as if Ella needed to be told how a woman in love should behave – she and Jake were on their own.

On our own and nothing is forbidden, her fox whispered in her mind.

She tried shaking the thought out of her head. Some things had to remain forbidden. But as long as she could refrain from a mating bite, she could get through the coming week, right?

Maybe even enjoy a moment or two, her fox added with a sultry swipe of her tail.

"Ever flown business before?" Jake murmured.

"Nope," she said, counting rows until she located their seats. Once they were settled in, she pulled out Lily's notes.

"What's that?" Jake asked in that smooth, low voice that made her toes curl.

"Orders." She stabbed the first item on the list with her index finger. "Number one. Cute, cuddly behavior on the plane and in public at all times." She frowned at the way Lily had penciled over and underlined *at all times*. "You think you're capable of cute and cuddly?"

The corners of Jake's mouth curled up. "Not sure we got that in Ranger training."

Definitely not. Ella shook her head, which somehow turned into resting her cheek comfortably on Jake's shoulder. He slid an arm around her and let his fingers play lightly over the fabric of her sundress.

"It is a nice dress," he murmured. A second later, he added, "Honey."

She stuck her elbow into his ribs, and he chuckled at her halfhearted protest.

The flight was too short to give the flight attendant much time to lavish attention on them, thank goodness, so it was just complimentary champagne — in real glasses, no less — and an embarrassing round of applause from all the passengers on the plane.

"Happy honeymoon," everyone cheered.

Ella took a deep breath before clinking her glass to Jake's.

"To us," Jake murmured in a low, even tone.

"To us," she breathed, telling herself she was just playing a part.

Jake nodded toward the paper. "What else is on that list?"

She went over the next couple of lines in an uncertain whisper. "Moonlight walk on the beach."

"That doesn't sound so hard," Jake said.

It sounded far too easy, in fact.

"Two straws in one cocktail."

"Another easy one," he said.

Lying in the sand with your head in his lap was also on the list, followed by *lounging by the poolside holding hands.* Ella looked up from the list. "Listen, Jake. We need to talk about th—"

He cut her off with a gentle finger to the lips, glancing around in a hint that they could be overheard. "I know. We have to talk about a lot of things. But not here. Not now." Then he spoke in a louder voice. "Wow. I can't believe we're really going to Maui."

"Me neither," she chimed in, playing the game as best she could. She wasn't one to giggle or flip her hair as Lily's list suggested, but she might be able to pull this off, after all.

She looked out the window. They definitely had to talk. But for now...

As the plane rose, she gazed out at the ocean. She had flown to Maui to help out at Koa Point on various occasions over the past months, but she tried looking at the view with honeymooner eyes this time. Jake looked too, leaning into her space, smelling incredibly good. Like leather and spruce and a tiny hint of lavender.

So good, her fox sighed.

Then she caught herself. This was work, not a honeymoon, and she'd better remember that.

She lowered her voice again. "What did Kai tell you?"

Jake pulled a paper from his pocket and unfolded the tight wad. Ella hid a smile. That was one of Jake's little idiosyncrasies, one she remembered the guys poking fun of at a desert camp one night.

He unfolded the paper and tilted it toward her.

"Now that's different," she murmured.

Kai's list was the opposite of Lily's, with points like *check for weaknesses in perimeter, calculate distances to possible sniper positions,* and *background checks on all guests.*

Jake nodded and put the paper away. "I figure, for tonight, we can focus on Lily's list." A second later, he hastened to add, "I mean, while we're in public."

He blushed, and her cheeks heated at the suggestion of what a newly wedded couple would get up to in the honeymoon suite on their first night of holy matrimony.

Ella puffed a breath upward, trying to cool off. "In public. Of course."

Which they did a surprisingly good job with throughout the short flight to Maui and as they waited for their outlandish number of bags on the other end. Ella made a face as the first few rolled out. Not one could be strapped to her back or attached to her thigh as she was used to from missions behind enemy lines. None of the contents would fit in the draining pockets of her cargo pants. Which, she supposed, was a good thing, considering those pants were buried deep in that luggage somewhere.

"Hey, I can get it," she muttered as Jake plucked the biggest suitcase off the belt with one hand. "Wait a second." She shoved her hands to her hips as he loaded it onto their trolley. "You didn't pull that *I'm a gentleman helping a lady* bullshit in the army. Why now?"

He shrugged and beat her to yet another bag. "Because doing it then could have affected how the other guys saw you." He placed the suitcase beside the others and motioned around. "Now, no one's watching — judging — what a girl can and can't do." He put air quotes around *girl*. "But now, I figure I'm allowed to do like my mom taught me." He finished with a wry smile. "Well, she tried. I'm not sure she succeeded."

Oh, she'd succeeded, all right, and Ella's heart just about melted. It had been an ongoing struggle to prove herself as one of the guys — not so much to the elite, all-shifter unit she'd belonged to, but to other soldiers they had come into contact with. Some of those men had gone out of their way to make her miserable, while others had naïvely offered help, which had only accomplished the opposite. Yet Jake had understood and respected that without ever saying a word.

"You want to push the trolley?" he offered.

She laughed and shoved him. "You push it, McBride."

"Yes, ma'am."

He grinned all the way through the arrivals building then waved to a burly Hawaiian who held a sign that had to have been prepared by Lily. *Mr. and Mrs. McBride. Happy Honeymoon!* it screamed in huge letters surrounded by little pink hearts.

"Mr. and Mrs. McBride?" the big *kanaka* asked.

Jake gave a friendly but firm shake of his head — not quite a yes, not quite a no. "Mr. McBride and Ms. Kitt."

The driver laughed and waggled his hand in a hang-loose sign. *"Aloha i Maui."*

He led them to a ridiculously overstretched limo and started loading up their luggage. Jake helped, and Ella did too, grabbing the biggest suitcase before anyone else could.

"You got a hell of a lot of power for such a little thing," the driver chuckled.

Ella was about to retort when Jake growled, "She's not little."

The driver stuck his hands up in the air and backed off with a laugh. "Not complaining, *brah*. She can load all the luggage she wants."

So she did, damn it, and minutes later, they were rolling across central Maui, heading back over the road they had driven that morning. But instead of continuing to the end of Honoapi'ilani Highway to Koa Point, the driver turned left at the imposing gates of the Kapa'akea Resort.

Jake let out a low whistle as they passed the polo grounds and golf course, and Ella swiveled her head in every direction when they entered the lavishly decorated lobby, starting her surveillance right away. She counted entrances, people, and stairways, making mental notes to explore every twisting hallway. Two men lounged by the windows, one reading a newspaper, the other checking his laptop. The restaurant was to the right, check-in to the left. A waiter hurried toward the bar with a tray loaded with drinks and—

She winced as he tripped over a fold in the rug. The ear-splitting noise of a dozen shattering glasses filled the room, and everyone looked up.

"Hey," Ella yelped as a heavy weight shoved her toward the floor. "What the—"

She cut herself off, finding herself in Jake's arms, a foot away from actually hitting the carpet. "Jake..."

He had caught himself just short of pulling her to the ground for cover. His eyes were wide, as if that had been incoming enemy fire and not a tray of glasses. The vein in his neck pulsed. And, shit. Now that everyone had looked away from the waiter, they were staring at her and Jake.

"Oh, gosh, these heels," she said, making a show of examining her shoes. "Thanks for grabbing me, honey."

The other guests turned away, smiling indulgently at the cute couple in love — which sure beat pitying looks of *What the hell is wrong with that guy?*

"I'm such a klutz," she went on, clutching his arm. Straightening, she squeezed his hand and whispered out of the side of her mouth. "It's okay. I know how it is."

Jake's blue eyes were dull with shame but grateful too, and she hurried to the check-in desk to put the awkward moment behind them.

"We're so happy to welcome another pair of happy honeymooners here," the receptionist gushed.

Ella stroked Jake's arm, wishing she could send her thoughts straight into his mind. Something like, *Everything is okay. Everything is all right.*

Jake stood stiff and still, but as they went through the check-in formalities, his tension slowly eased.

Just like I said, her fox murmured. *Our mate needs us.*

Ella took a deep breath. She'd witnessed Tessa calm Kai down in a similar way and watched Dawn chase the haunted look out of Hunter's eyes. It was amazing, the effect a destined mate had on her partner.

She bit her lip as the crux of the problem hit her all over again. Tessa and Dawn hadn't risked killing the men they loved when they'd completed the mating ritual. But Jake...

"You'll find a complimentary bottle of champagne chilling in your room." The receptionist's eyes twinkled.

Ella closed her eyes, trying not to picture a king-size bed covered with rose petals in an ocean-view suite that screamed *Sex!*

Maybe this wasn't such a good idea, after all.

"On behalf of everyone here at the Kapa'akea Resort, we wish you a wonderful honeymoon. If there's anything we can do to make your stay more comfortable, please let us know."

Ella glanced at the exit, but, shit. Too late to rethink this insane plan.

Jake took the key when she didn't. "Thanks."

The receptionist motioned a bellhop over. "Toby, the bags, please."

Toby looked to be one of those *just out of college, not quite sure what I'm doing with my life* guys who'd never hefted a weapon or looked a deadly enemy in the eye. But it was hard to resent his eager, puppy dog innocence, and his mile-a-minute chatter helped dispel the last of Jake's uneasiness.

"I'm actually a valet, but I'm moonlighting as a bellhop," Toby said as the elevator dinged through one floor after another. "So I'm moving up in the world." He laughed. "You get it?"

Ella winced at the pun. "Got it."

"So, you're honeymooners, huh? We get a lot of weddings here. You should've seen the one we had not too long ago. Regina Vanderpelt. You've heard of her, right?"

Ella sighed. She'd heard the stories, all right.

"Craziest wedding ever, especially since the bride called it off at the last minute. The cool part was I got to ride in a Rolls-Royce!"

The elevator dinged and came to a stop on the second-to-last floor.

"Here we are." Toby motioned to a gold-fringed door at the end of the hall, swiped a keycard over the touchpad, and pushed the door open with a flourish.

"Welcome to the honeymoon suite. Have a great time!"

Ella edged in then froze. The suite was amazing, but what made her pulse rush was the sight of the bed in the room to the right.

King-size. Ivory-colored silk sheets strewn with rose petals. Yep. That definitely screamed *Sex!*

"What do you think?" Jake asked.

Ella kept her mouth shut, but her fox hummed inside. *I love it.*

Chapter Seven

It's okay. I know how it is.

Jake replayed Ella's words as he made a makeshift bed of the couch — which totally defeated the point of a honeymoon suite, but he was too keyed up to think much about that. All he could think of were Ella's words.

I know how it is.

That was the amazing thing — that Ella really understood. A couple of whispered words from her was all it took to make him go from feeling like a nutcase to letting a little bit of hope creep back into his soul. The feeling that it wasn't so crazy for him to short-circuit from time to time. That maybe, just maybe. . .

"You sure you don't want the bed?" Ella asked, breaking in to his thoughts.

He looked up. Oh, he wanted the bed, all right. But only if she was sleeping there too. And Ella was offering to swap, not inviting him in.

She stood in the bedroom doorway wearing a yellow sleep shirt that went halfway to her knees — another new look for her.

He rubbed a thumb against his bare chest as she twirled a lock of her long hair. Maybe he wasn't the only one figuring himself out these days. But, crap. If settling back into civilian life meant getting over a hump, he still had a long, slow climb ahead. So even if by some miracle Ella invited him to share the bed, he'd better say no. He was still too edgy, too unsettled. Too likely to wake up sweaty from a nightmare.

"The couch is fine, thanks." He threw a sheet into place, wondering if Ella minded him wearing only a pair of boxers.

Or even better, if she liked that look as much as he liked hers.

"Well, then. Good night, McBride." She clicked off the lights.

"Good night, Kitt," he said, making sure it didn't come out in a horny growl.

He slipped into his makeshift bed and stared at the ceiling, steeling himself for what was sure to come the moment he fell asleep. Explosions. Screams. Bloodied faces. All that mixed with the image of Manny's lifeless body in an auto body shop.

I'm telling you, man. Someone is taking us out, one by one. Hoover's haunted voice echoed through his mind.

Hoover had always been on the paranoid side, but Manny's death made three in a row for his unit. Chalsmith's accident hadn't seemed suspicious at the time, and neither had Junger's climbing mishap. But a bullet in the head in broad daylight and a homicidal car speeding along the road on Maui... Maybe Hoover was right.

One of us is next, man. And I swear, it ain't gonna be me.

Jake rolled, trying to distract himself by listening to the sound of the ocean. Ella had left the balcony doors open, letting the sea breeze waft in, stirring the curtains quietly.

He closed and opened his eyes a few times, testing how close the nightmares might lie. Lately, they had taken longer than usual to set in, as if the nightmares had to track him down on an island in the middle of the Pacific first. He looked at the stars for a few minutes then shut his eyes again, hoping for a little undisturbed sleep before the ugly images began.

And the strangest thing happened. He slept. Just... slept. Not a single nightmare. No tossing and turning. No wild fantasies about Ella either. Just a solid night's sleep. He must have, because the next time he opened his eyes, it was dawn.

He blinked a few times and rolled at a nearby sound. It was Ella, padding quietly by on her way to the balcony, where she gazed at the view. Her hair was mussed, her face still creased with pillow lines, her feet bare on the tile floor. A single word popped into his mind.

Pretty.

Make that, *really pretty.*

The first time he'd met Ella, he'd noticed her beauty. A totally off-limits, understated beauty no man could miss. But he'd never thought of Ella as *pretty* because that word had *feminine* and *off guard* woven into it.

But, wow. There she was. A little pensive, maybe, but a long way from *warrior princess*, for sure.

"Sleep well?" he murmured, coming up to one elbow.

She turned and opened her mouth to reply but got stuck there for a moment. Her eyes traveled up and down his body before she hauled them back to his face and nodded quickly. "I did sleep well. You?"

He nodded casually, as if a good night's sleep hadn't come as a surprise. Maybe the salt air had helped. In which case, he would have to rethink the *settle down on a quiet ranch* plan.

Ella's nostrils flared, and it hit him. Maybe sleeping better wasn't a function of being on Maui. Maybe it came from being close to her.

"I'll be right back," he muttered, heading to the bathroom before she caught the dumbstruck look on his face. He started a slow, pensive shower — then hurried up to finish and dress when he realized Ella hadn't had her chance yet. But she didn't seem in any rush when he rejoined her on the balcony.

"So," she said. "I guess we ought to start working on those lists."

"Good idea," he mumbled, trying not to stare at her long, smooth legs.

She strode inside and returned with two coffee mugs and the two lists, laying them out on the outdoor coffee table. He slid in beside her on the outdoor couch, hyperaware of how close their thighs were.

"Okay, so... breakfast first," Ella said then made a face. "Cozy couple stuff."

He frowned as if he hated the idea too.

She tapped *background checks on all guests* on the other list. "I could hang around the dining room and keep my ears open after breakfast while you go find Toby."

He lifted an eyebrow. "The bellhop? He seems pretty clueless to me."

"Sure, but he sees everyone coming and going. You never know. Let's see what we can pick up from talkative staff to get a handle on who's here and what's going on. You know — strange behavior, unexpected guests, anonymous bookings. That kind of thing." Then she frowned, looking back at Lily's list. "Then I guess we'll have to go to the beach."

"Damn."

She swatted his shoulder.

"Hey, it could be worse." He pointed out.

She looked at the view over the edge of her coffee mug then let her eyes slide over to him. "Could be worse," she agreed.

"Remember that base camp in Zaranj?"

Her laugh was music to his ears, and she held her mug out for a toast. "True. What we wouldn't have given for all this back there."

He tapped his mug against hers, relishing a moment that was neither awkward guy-girl thing nor sweaty soldier cama- raderie, but somewhere in between. It lasted a good minute too, before Ella stood, stretched, and headed for the shower, murmuring, "Gotta get ready."

Jake tried not to picture her naked in the shower — he re- ally did. He also tried not to imagine Ella tipping her head back and working shampoo into her hair — or better yet, tipping her head back and letting him do that. He tried not imagining a lot of things but failed on pretty much every count.

Watching a fishing boat steam toward the horizon didn't help, so he tore a car rental flier into tiny bits, mixed them up, and reassembled them like a puzzle. Again and again, a little too obsessively for his own liking, but what else could he do?

When Ella came out of the shower, he worked hard not to look up. Not that he would have seen much with her behind the half-closed bedroom door. But his ears tuned in to the sound of rustling fabric and the tap of her feet across the floor. The faint scent of shampoo tickled his nose, setting off those fantasies all over again.

"Ready," she said, pushing the door open.

For a second, he gaped. He'd never seen Ella in a cute, floral print shorts-shirt combo like that before. A second later, he schooled his face into a neutral expression because, wow. The shorts showed a hell of a lot of leg, and the blue tones made her coppery-brown eyes look twice as bright.

"Ready," he mumbled.

"I'd better fix this." Ella turned back to the bed and twisted the sheets to make it look like a couple of honeymooners had spent the night there, shredding his fantasies.

Business, McBride. He sighed, pulling the sheet off the couch. *Pure business.*

Luckily, *business* included sliding a hand around her waist the second they stepped out the door.

"Loving couple, remember?" He tried to look apologetic.

"Loving couple," Ella said in a completely flat tone.

But her body stayed warm and cozy against his side all the way downstairs and throughout breakfast, and her eyes rarely left his. *Cozy couple* was working — too well, at times. Her fingers played over his as the two of them lingered over coffee and croissants, and she didn't jerk away when their legs bumped under the table. But just when things threatened to slip from *cozy* to *steamy* — like when her hand slid from an easy resting position on his knee to higher on his thigh — Ella jerked away and shut down. It came with a flash in her eyes and an under-her-breath mutter, as if she were mad at someone for making her do that.

"Okay, find Toby," she ordered, and just like that, they ricocheted from happy honeymooners to calculating PIs.

Toby, as it turned out, was just as talkative as the previous night, but nothing in his chatter threw up a red flag.

"Anything?" Ella whispered when Jake caught up with her in the rose garden an hour later.

"Nothing. You?"

"Nothing." She sighed. "I guess it's time to go to the beach."

"Damn."

They changed into swim gear — which, in Ella's case, meant a turquoise bikini that nearly made his jaw unhinge — and spent an hour in lounge chairs within earshot of the beach bar. They made quite a pair — her with her tattoos, him with his scraped-up legs — who cared? An hour passed, and though they didn't pick up on any critical information, they did tick *two straws in one cocktail* off Lily's list. Afterward, they took a long walk, pretending to admire the scenery while checking for weak points in the resort's outer walls.

"What is it?" Ella asked.

Jake glared at a white sedan that revved out of the parking lot, going much too fast. It was impossible to tell one rental from another, but they all looked like possible killing machines.

Someone is taking us out. . .

Maybe he ought to get in touch with Hoover, after all.

"Nothing," he said quickly, pushing the paranoia aside.

Four more days passed in the same not-quite-relaxed way. Days were divided and subdivided by the tasks on their contrasting lists. Nights were quiet — very quiet — with each of them self-consciously tucked into a separate bed. From time to time, the happy couple act worked so well, he forgot it was an act. Ella seemed to forget too, and they'd end up sidling closer, touching, gazing into each other's eyes. But every time Jake was sure Ella would open up to him — really open up — she'd do that blink/jerk away/mutter thing and consult Kai's list.

"Calculate distances to possible sniper positions," she announced, sending him off in one direction while she set off in the other.

He started to wonder if Ella had her own particular, dual-personality form of PTSD. But maybe she was walking the same tightwire he was, careening from *I need you in my life* to *You deserve better than me.*

"Crap." Ella scowled at her phone after breakfast on the fourth day.

Jake looked around. They hadn't discovered any signs of mischief so far. Had she noticed something?

"Everything okay?"

Ella nodded quickly and spoke in a hushed tone. "Hunter was supposed to take care of something today, but I have to go instead."

"Go where?"

Her eyes drifted across the sprawling resort and focused on a point far away. "Pu'u Pu'eo," she said in a wistful tone.

"Pu'u what?"

She waved in a vague way. "The place where I grew up. Where we all grew up, actually — Hunter and Kai and me. Georgia Mae left the property to us. We never wanted to let it go, but it's getting so overgrown..." She fidgeted with her napkin and scuffed the floor. "None of us has time to check on it, and it hurts to see the place neglected like that. So we agreed to sell, and the realtor just called with an interested party." She sighed. "I guess selling the place is a good thing, but... well, you know."

That achy, *time to let go of the past* feeling? Yeah, he knew all too well.

She scowled at the phone. "The realtor has someone coming to look at it this afternoon, but they'll barely be able to walk onto the property, it's so overgrown. Hunter can't go to clear a path, and Kai has to spend most of the day here setting up the extra security that's set to arrive today. So that leaves me."

He corrected her immediately. "That leaves *us*."

The grateful look on her face made his fantasies tiptoe a little closer again, and he grinned.

"Seriously?" she asked, brightening.

Jake bit back *I would go to the end of the world and back for you.* "Sure. Might even be fun."

"Fun?" Her eyebrows shot up. "You should see the place, McBride. It will be hard work. None of this lazing around next to the pool stuff. You think you can handle that?"

He grinned. "I believe I can."

Chapter Eight

Jake couldn't understand why he felt like a jailbird set free when they hit the road. Maybe because high-end places like the Kapa'akea Resort weren't exactly his thing. Pulling on boots instead of loafers felt good, and Ella seemed just as happy for a change of scenery too. In no time, they had changed into comfortable work clothes, rented a Jeep, and headed out.

"I guess this does keep with the brief," Ella said as she fired up the engine and drove down the long, palm-lined drive of the resort. "We can make it look like a day trip to Haleakala or Hana, and Kai will have the resort covered as he sets up the extra security guys."

"Just don't let any of the guys see this Jeep," Jake joked as they made the right turn onto the main road. The Jeep was bright pink, which went a long way in reminding him this wasn't another army mission in some godforsaken corner of the world. The coast whipped by to his right, looking just like a travel ad. The sun warmed his face, and the wind pulled at his hair. It felt like one of those rare days off from an assignment that had dragged on for too long.

"I thought the surf out here was big." He waved at a strip of beach where tourists tottered on surfboards in tiny little waves.

Ella laughed. "At this time of year, all the action is over on the Hana side."

"You grew up on Maui, right?"

She nodded briskly. "I moved here after my mom died."

He sucked in a breath. Shit. "Sorry."

Ella waved like it was nothing, but her face tensed. She fingered her necklace, making the silver glint in the sun, and he wondered if it had been her mother's, once upon a time. "Maui was a great place to grow up. But somehow..."

"Somehow?" he prompted after a few seconds went by.

"Don't get me wrong — I loved it here, and I loved Georgia Mae, my foster mother. But something always pulled me back to the Southwest. There's just something about the landscape, I guess. How rugged it is. How quiet."

He nodded. Yeah, he knew just what she meant.

"When other girls went from decorating their rooms with unicorns to boy band posters, I was decorating mine with pictures of the Southwest." She lifted one hand from the steering wheel and drew shapes in the air. "Canyons. Mesas. Cliff dwellings. All that kind of stuff."

He nodded along. Maui was beautiful, but he longed for the West, too. All that sky, that space. Space enough to allow a guy to get lost in his thoughts — and maybe even find himself again.

"Is that where you've been since you got back stateside?" he asked.

"Yep. Arizona. I was born there. Got myself a good job on a ranch." Her voice grew a little wistful, her focus not entirely on the road. "A big place that runs cattle and goats. Tons and tons of space... You would like it there."

Jake was just starting to nod when Ella corrected herself abruptly. "I mean, I like it there."

He watched her from the corner of his eye. Did part of her soul wish he were part of her life? If he were honest with himself, he'd admit that he was starting to picture her into his life the same way.

The road bent away from the coast, and Ella changed the subject. "You're from Colorado, right? Ever thought of going back?"

Jake's lips tightened. "I did go back."

Ella didn't say anything, and he figured he would leave it at that. But something spurred him to explain. After all, Ella wasn't like everyone else. She understood him — really understood him. So he went on after a pause.

"My older brother took over the family ranch. Dad died while I was gone, and my mom moved to Tucson where her sister lives."

Ella tilted her head in one of those *so what happened?* looks.

"I guess I was thinking it would all be the way I left it." The landscape blurred as he stared off into the distance. "My brother and his wife took over the main house. She redecorated and everything. I guess it was high time, but..." He waved a hand vaguely. "Anyway, it's their place now. Which I guess is a good thing. It kind of forced me to move on."

He decided to leave out the part about not really having anywhere to move on to.

"I was staying with friends when Boone called with this job. But someday, when I get the chance, a job at a ranch would be nice."

They drove in silence for the next fifteen minutes, when Ella hit the blinker and pulled over into a parking lot. There was a hardware store there, a tire and lube place, and a lunch truck in the lee of a couple of Norfolk pines.

"I need to grab a few things," Ella said, getting out of the car. "Oh, and it would be good to pick up sandwiches. There's nothing out by the property."

He nodded. "I'll get the sandwiches. Chicken with sharp mustard for you?"

Her eyes went wide.

Yes, he wanted to say. *I have been paying attention.*

Even so, he was surprised by all the details he was able to recall once he thought about it. Like how she liked her coffee — black and sweet — and how dark she liked her toast. How she crossed her right leg over her left and tilted her head while fiddling with her hair. He even knew which side she preferred sleeping on — the left. All the little things he hadn't had time to learn about her before, he'd been memorizing now.

He cleared his throat. Damn. Either he had an unhealthy obsession, or he was head over heels in love.

"Chicken with mustard would be perfect," Ella said quietly.

He scuffed his boot over asphalt and nodded. "Perfect."

She disappeared into the hardware store, leaving him to head for the lunch truck. There was one guy in line and an older woman in the shade nearby, peddling an eclectic collection of goods — everything from beaded necklaces to kitchen magnets and other knickknacks.

"Palm reading. Tarot cards. See your future?"

Jake made a face. He wasn't sure he'd like what he would see. But his gaze caught on a small wooden box, and he couldn't resist stepping over for a better look.

"It's an antique," the woman said.

Which meant he probably couldn't afford it, but heck. He'd already picked up the wooden box and turned it over in his hands. It wasn't much bigger than a cigar box, but taller and inlaid with several types of wood.

"That's whalebone there." The woman pointed. "The real thing."

He pulled gently on an engraved knob but nothing happened, and the woman cackled. "It's a puzzle box. You can't just open it. You have to figure it out."

Now, he was really intrigued.

The lid was inlaid with tiles of different types — some teak, some beech, others mahogany, plus a couple of ivory squares — like the top of one of those puzzle cubes. There was one open space, and he slid the ivory piece left, moving it into a new column.

"What's inside?" He tested the weight in his hands.

The copper-skinned woman smiled sadly. "Destiny."

His eyes wandered to the hardware store doors, peeking at Ella between the aisles. Destiny. What would his be?

"What can I get you?" the lunch truck guy called, and Jake jerked away.

"One chicken with spicy mustard, one roast beef."

He tapped his foot and peeked into the hardware store again. Ella was in one of the aisles, weighing machetes against each other and testing the blades with her thumb. She even gave one a few test swings, scaring the hell out of an older guy in the neighboring aisle.

Jake chuckled. Ella was Ella. Warrior. Tomboy. But, damn. She made a perfect gorgeous honeymooner, too.

As he paid and waited for the sandwiches, his eyes drifted over to that box again.

"Ready to go?" Ella called, striding across the lot.

"Ready," he said, though his eyes stayed on the vendor's table.

"What?" Ella stepped over.

He hemmed and hawed a little, and her eyes followed his. He could see the exact moment Ella noticed the puzzle box among all the other items on the cluttered table. Her eyes sparkled, and she broke into a grin. "Oh, that's you, McBride."

And just like that, he had his wallet out and his hand on the box.

"Sixty dollars," the vendor said.

"Sixty?" Ella protested.

Jake would have been content to slap down sixty bucks — he wasn't much of a haggler, not even after years of missions in far-flung corners the world where bargaining was built into every price. But Ella...

"Twenty-five," she said, staring the woman down.

"Fifty."

"Thirty."

And so it went, with Jake looking back and forth like a spectator at a tennis match. Finally, Ella nodded in satisfaction and shook with the old woman. "Thirty-seven."

He hid a smile. No one got the better of Ella. No one.

He paid before either of the two tough-talking women changed their minds and ended up playing with the puzzle box for the rest of the drive. A pleasant drive, actually, once Ella quit teasing him about that box.

"Hoping to find treasure, McBride?"

He grinned. The box was even better than a regular puzzle, what with all the different tabs and sliding panels that interlocked.

"Nah. Just finding my inner child," he insisted, shaking it next to his ear and then trying a different combination.

"Won't have to look far to find that." She grinned.

"Watch the road, Kitt," he shot back.

They drove in easy silence for the next few minutes. Now and then, Ella pointed something out. There was a giant volcano called Haleakala and the hulking wreck of an old sugar mill. Not long after that, the road went from highway to twisty, turny country lane, following a jagged coastline high over the crashing surf.

"This is the windward side of Maui. The road to Hana — it's a little town all the way down there." She waved forward. "A lot of people drive out here just for the views. Our place is just up that slope."

She lifted one finger from the steering wheel to point, and Jake caught a glimpse of red blossoms erupting from a tall stand of trees.

"African flame trees," Ella murmured with a faraway look in her eyes.

Not long after, she slowed and turned onto a dirt road where she switched to four-wheel drive and maneuvered the vehicle deftly around several steep, rocky curves.

Jake hung on to the dashboard while the vehicle lurched and bounced. "Now I know why you insisted on renting a Jeep. You lived way out here?"

Ella laughed. "We sure did. Lots of privacy."

He ducked to avoid an overhanging vine, and every time the engine stopped straining for a moment or two, he caught the sound of singing birds and crashing water.

"My favorite waterfall is down there." Ella waved to the left.

Her *favorite* waterfall — like there were many more. And maybe there were, judging by the lush scenery and plunging cliffs. Then Ella turned a tight corner and squeaked to a stop in front of a crooked metal gate made of old pipes.

"This is it." She grabbed the machetes and slid out of the car.

Jake watched from over her shoulder as she jiggled a rusty lock and finally pushed the gate open. A dozen vines went with it, hanging on like so many aging sentries. Apparently, there was no need to repark the Jeep – and no place to fit it on the overgrown property. Jake couldn't imagine too many people came up the rough drive.

"Whoa." He ducked as something swooped over his head.

Ella laughed. "Pu'eo."

"Pu-what-o?"

"An owl. They live around here. Some old friends, you might say." She chuckled and started hacking her way through the waist-high grass. "Come on."

The owl fluttered to a branch high overhead and peered at Jake skeptically. Every step he took, the bird followed with watchful eyes.

Ella motioned around with her machete. "Papaya... Banana... We had a whole grove here." Her voice went from excited to wistful and back again. "Avocado too. We had to take turns fetching water from the creek. Kind of rustic, I guess you could say, but it suited us just fine."

Then she stopped abruptly and stared at the house. The shine gradually faded from her eyes, and her shoulders hunched a tiny bit. The little cottage that stood on low stilts had a lot of character, but the white paint was chipped, and broken shards of glass hung in one of the windowpanes. The steps were crooked, each slanting in a different direction as jungle rot set in. One of the sheets of corrugated iron protecting the roof had slipped a foot or two.

Jake put a hand on Ella's shoulder. No *cozy couple* act this time, just the kind of reassuring touch she had given him the night of Hoover's call. The place was a mess, and he could feel her pain. Still, it didn't take much imagination to picture a younger Ella running down the sloping property or kicking a ball around. Flowerpots and wood carvings circled the place, hinting at pride and love.

"Nice," he said without a hint of irony. "A nice place to grow up."

Ella's chest rose and fell in a silent sigh. "It was nice. But it's time to let go." She straightened her shoulders and nodded to the right. "You start over there. I'll start over here, okay? Maybe by the time the realtor gets here, we can make it look less like a jungle and more like a yard."

"Yes, ma'am."

"Quit ma'aming me, McBride."

He grinned. "Yes, ma'am."

Within a sweaty hour or two, they had hacked the creeping jungle back and succeeded in making the grass look more like a lawn. Then they swept out the house, raked leaves off the porch, and dragged the biggest branches littering the lawn into a neat stack. Ella spent a long time fussing over a sunny bedroom at the back that must have been her own, but when she came out, she was as businesslike as ever. Maybe even more so. She washed the dusty windows with some water she'd hauled from the creek while Jake straightened a droopy shutter and got that roof panel in place.

Finally, they stood back and admired their work. They were scratched, pouring sweat, and sporting countless mosquito bites, but the place looked a lot better.

"Feels good," Ella said, making him laugh.

She was right, though. Physical work always felt good. The times where you concentrated on heaving and hauling instead of the shit inside your head. Jake tilted his face toward the sun, imagining a place to work the land and make an honest living. A place to grow old with no regrets.

When he opened his eyes, they slid right to Ella, and the words echoed in his mind. *No regrets.*

He stepped closer, clearing his throat, intent on saying something. *Ella, we need to talk.* Or *Ella, come over, sit down, and hear me out. Please.*

She looked up and caught her breath as if she sensed what was coming.

"Listen, Ella," he started.

But just when he'd worked out where to start, the sound of a straining engine growled, and they both snapped their heads toward the road.

"That must be them," Ella murmured, stepping past him after a pause.

Jake studied his boots for a good ten seconds before puffing out his cheeks and looking up again. Ella was already stomping over to the gate in her no-nonsense stride and waving when the

74

realtor stepped out of the passenger side of a red SUV. But the moment the driver's door opened, she froze in her tracks.

Jake caught up and watched as a big, burly man unfolded himself from the driver's seat. First, Jake saw a long, thick leg clad in army pants, then a hairy arm, wide as a branch, and finally, a smooth, shaved head and a face wearing a wicked grin.

"Here's the place I was telling you about," the realtor said, but Jake's attention stayed on the big guy. He seemed familiar in a way Jake couldn't exactly place — and dangerous.

Ella's nostrils flared, and Jake saw her eyes narrow in suspicion. Did she know that guy or did she just get the same bad feeling he did?

"Three-bedroom bungalow surrounded by virgin forest," the realtor continued, slipping a pair of sunglasses over his thinning hair.

Jake immediately dismissed the realtor. That slick white guy in a loud Hawaiian shirt wasn't a threat. That big guy, on the other hand, had a malicious, intrusive air about him.

The realtor waved around without bothering to introduce Ella to his customer. As if she were part of the landscape, not someone to be addressed.

"You got your banana trees, your avocado..."

Ella's banana trees and avocado, Jake wanted to say. He widened his stance and planted himself firmly in the way of the bustling realtor, who finally looked up.

"Oh. You must be Hunter Bjornvald."

Jake jerked his head in a no, keeping his eyes on the big guy who hung back a little, appraising the scene. He stood a solid six foot five, towering over the realtor and sniffing the breeze much like Ella did.

"She's in charge here," Jake grunted, nodding at Ella.

The realtor looked at Ella in surprise, and Jake had to fight back a growl. What would it be like to have to deal with that all the time? Ella was as tenacious and capable as the toughest Marine, but guys like these often didn't look past her compact frame.

"Oh, Miss Kitt. Right?"

Ella folded her arms across her chest, glaring at the new-comer. Lumbering up deliberately, the man gave them plenty of time to appreciate his enormous size. He had the build of a weightlifter, with slabs of muscle chiseled over his legs, torso, and arms. When he smiled at Ella, the points of his canines showed.

"Gideon Goode," the big man rumbled. His face was friendly, but his eyes were dark. "Mind if I have a look around?"

Yes, I do mind, Jake nearly said, but it wasn't his place. Too bad, because he already distrusted the guy. Eyes didn't lie, and those eyes were appraising. Scheming. Plotting. First, they swept over the property. But when those dark eyes drifted over to Jake, the man's jaw tightened, and his eyes sparked with what looked like hate. A moment later, those dark eyes dulled to a more neutral expression and moved on to Ella, brightening with interest.

The owl fluttered in the tree, shifting around in unease. Jake felt the same way. Gideon Goode. Did he know that guy? And, damn. What was up with him?

Ella glared at Goode for a full five seconds before stepping aside and gritting her teeth. "Go ahead. Have a look."

Jake watched closely, hanging back with Ella while the re-altor and Goode wandered around the house.

"You know that guy?" he muttered out of the side of his mouth.

"No," Ella grunted. "But I know his type."

She didn't say more, but there was definitely something going on. Ella practically growled when the man stomped up the stairs and entered the house. A minute later, he came out, shaking his head.

"Not what I had in mind," he said with an apologetic smile that didn't reach his eyes.

Good riddance, the owl in the tree seemed to say with a flutter of its wings. It watched closely as Goode and the realtor walked back to the car.

"No problem. I've got another place you'll love," the realtor said.

Goode barely nodded, studying Jake with those dark, vengeful eyes as he went. Or was that a trick of the light? Goode's gaze darted to Ella, back to Jake, and over to Ella again, taking on the greedy sheen of a poacher.

Jake bristled. *Watch it, asshole. She's mine.*

The dark eyes grew amused, then scheming, examining Ella in a whole new way. Running his eyes up and down her body. Baiting Jake, for sure.

Jake stepped forward. Whoever the guy was, he was about to get his ass kicked.

Goode smiled as if that was just what he'd wanted. He opened his mouth to speak, but the realtor reached across the car and tapped the horn in a jaunty, *beep-beep!*

"Ready to go?"

Goode gave Jake one more long, menacing look-over before his eyes dropped back to Ella. "Nice to have met you, Miss Kitt."

She jutted her chin, unimpressed. "Good luck finding a house."

She didn't sound all too sincere, and Jake couldn't blame her.

Asshole, he let his eyes say, and the man finally turned away. The SUV creaked on its struts when the big guy got in. Throughout most of the awkward twelve-point turn it took to get out of that narrow space, Goode kept his eyes on Ella. Finally, he pushed the car into first gear and disappeared around the bend.

Jake and Ella stood still as statues for a full minute after the sound of the car faded. Gradually, the birds that had gone silent started singing and whistling again, and the charged atmosphere relaxed a little. But something still felt off.

"Goode, huh?" Jake murmured in disgust.

Ella snorted. "Goode. Yeah, right."

Chapter Nine

Ella's fox was snarling, snapping, and growling inside long after the realtor and his customer had gone.

Goode, my ass, her inner beast snarled.

She had smelled shifter even before the two men reached the gate, though she couldn't pinpoint what kind. The realtor was just a human, and an annoying one at that. But that Gideon guy... A shifter, for sure. Her mind whirled through the possibilities. A lion? Tiger? Some kind of feline. His scent didn't have that musky, jungle element Cruz's had, but he didn't have the open savanna feel of a lion shifter either. He did have the size, though. More than the size.

It's not the size of the dog in the fight. It's the size of the fight in the dog, her fox grunted as she stared at the empty road.

She would have liked a chance to challenge the guy, even though she didn't know exactly why. Maybe because he was so smug and cocky. The way his eyes had undressed her... Had that been to rile her up or to goad Jake?

She looked at Jake and found his eyes blazing as if he were a shifter too. She put a hand on his chest without thinking. Whether that was an unconscious attempt to calm herself or to calm Jake, she didn't know. But either way, it worked. The angry thump of Jake's heart slowed, and her pulse stopped revving too. She looked up at the house, trying to let anger go and love in, the way Georgia Mae had always told her to do.

Her fox snarled, still huffing and puffing inside. *Me and my mate. Together, we can take on anything. Anything.*

She frowned, because it didn't work that way. Jake was a tough soldier who could hold his own with any human – but to bring him into the shifter world would pit him against forces way out of his league.

A cardinal flitted over the freshly trimmed lawn in a flash of red, bringing her thoughts back to Gideon Goode. What was another shifter doing on Maui? Did Silas and the others know about him?

"I wouldn't have sold the property to that asshole anyway," she muttered.

Jake laughed and pulled her into a hug. "No way. You need to find someone who deserves this place. Someone who will make it a home. Really a home, not an address."

She closed her eyes. Jake got it. He really got it.

Of course he does, her fox sighed.

And, oops. She found herself locking her arms around his waist and hugging back. But damn, did that feel good. That *two of us against the world* feeling instead of having to deal with problems all on her own.

"Time to head back?" Jake whispered when she eased away.

She let her eyes rove over the crooked roof, the uneven steps, the unpicked fruit sagging from overladen branches.

I don't want to go, she wanted to say. *I want to bring it all back. Those innocent, happy times. The simplicity. The love.*

But all that had been a long time ago. Georgia Mae was gone, and Ella was all grown up.

We can have a life like that again. With Jake in a new home, her fox insisted, filling her mind with images of the desert Southwest.

"I just need a minute to call Hunter," she murmured before her fox got carried away.

Jake spent a few seconds studying her before he gave a satisfied nod and let her step away.

She dialed and paced impatiently until Hunter picked up the phone with his usual, rumbling, "Hello?"

She kept it short and sweet, speaking out loud for some parts and sending other thoughts directly into Hunter's mind. Their mental connection was tenuous over such a distance, but if she really concentrated, she could get her thoughts through.

"I need you to check out the jerk who came to see the property," she started, adding, *the jerk of a shifter who came to see the property.*

"A shifter?" Hunter barked over his end of the line. "What kind?"

"The kind I don't trust." *Some kind of feline. Didn't Silas mention a meeting with a delegation of lions?*

"I'll check it out," Hunter said.

A minute later, she ended the call, feeling slightly more settled than before. "Ready to go," she said, coming back to Jake.

"Are you sure?" He nodded at the house.

She turned in a slow circle, taking it all in one more time. Maybe she, Kai, and Hunter ought to reconsider selling the place.

"Ready," she said at last.

One of the owls hooted in farewell as they walked to the Jeep. The bird wasn't a shifter, but it had been a friend of Georgia Mae's, and its nods and flutters told Ella all she needed to know.

Home. This is home.

Okay, she would definitely talk to Kai and Hunter about keeping the place. But they'd have to get to that after things settled down, which could take a while.

She sighed and stepped into the Jeep, casting one more look around before driving down the road. A truck sped by as she waited at the intersection to the main road, followed by a rental with a white-knuckled tourist at the wheel, and finally, a rusty local pickup with the radio turned up loud enough to hear a soulful island tune. She turned onto the road behind it and fiddled with the radio knob until she found the same station.

"Nice song," Jake murmured.

"*Over the Rainbow*," she said. "Israel Kamakawiwo'ole." She'd heard that version more often than she could count, but she'd never tired of it. Somehow, that song managed to make her dream of both her homes — the desert and Maui. Before long, her fingers were tapping and her inner fox humming.

She caught Jake smiling at her, and she couldn't help grinning back. It was a nice picture – him in the passenger seat of the car, the wind playing in his hair, looking more settled with every winding mile.

Each song that came on the radio had her humming louder. They all seemed like one-time favorites, and the familiar chords made long-forgotten lyrics pop into her mind. Jake hummed and fiddled with the puzzle box, and her fox kept busy seeking peeks at him. It was nice seeing Jake like that. A little more relaxed, and somehow more lovable with every second that ticked by. It felt good to be two ordinary people driving into the sunset, humming and puzzling along. So good that she found herself wanting to stretch out the drive and hide from reality for a while.

The sun was kissing the horizon when they hit the West Maui coast, and before she knew it, she'd flicked the blinker on for a left turn into Puamana Beach Park.

"What's up?" Jake asked, looking around.

She motioned. "The sun is setting. It would be a shame to miss it, right?"

He nodded and spoke quietly. "Yeah, that would be a shame."

She pulled into a spot facing the water and sat back in the seat of that ridiculous pink Jeep, reaching for Jake's hand without thinking.

What are you doing? part of her mind screamed.

But Jake reached out at exactly the same time, and it was too nice to let go.

Really nice, her fox sighed.

"Kind of like real honeymooners, huh?" he murmured, squeezing her hand as the sun dropped lower, sending pink streaks over Lanai and Molokai.

She nodded. "Pretty close."

It was more than close, at least in one overly hopeful part of her mind.

We can take Jake back to Arizona, settle down on the ranch, and live happily ever after, her fox sighed.

82

So easy to imagine, especially with the sea breeze promising fair sailing and the sun shooting rays of brilliant color across the sky. But Arizona was so far away. . .

Don't forget. We have the honeymoon suite, her fox said in a naughty tone.

Ella kept her eyes on the horizon. God, it would be so nice to make the most of that place. Just for one night.

Just one night, her fox breathed.

Every morning, she crumpled the bedsheets to make it appear as if she and Jake were actually sleeping together, and another morning of that might just kill her.

I have a much better solution, her fox said, far too innocently.

I don't want to hear it. Ella shook her head.

But her fox plunged ahead with visions of steamy sex that made her ache with need. Visions of herself and Jake, finally giving in to carnal desire. She saw the two of them wrapped around each other in bed, missionary style, panting hard.

She took a sharp breath and stared straight ahead.

I'll cover security today, Kai had yelled in the background of Hunter's phone call earlier that day. *You guys take the night off before the big day. And make it count, honeymooners.*

Kai had been joking, but her fox kept up the sultry images, chipping away at her resistance. She imagined Jake and her on all fours, her clutching the sheets, him pumping hard from behind. Or her on top in reverse cowgirl, riding him hard. Or her spread wide on the bed, with Jake sliding over her body, exploring with his tongue. Lower and lower until he touched down on her sex, making fireworks shoot off in her mind.

Heat surged through her body, and she nearly groaned out loud.

"What did you say?" Jake asked, hauling her out of the fantasy.

She cleared her throat harshly, not daring to look his way. "Guess we ought to go," she murmured, revving the engine back to life and heading back to the road.

Damn it. Quit doing that, she ordered her fox.

Doing what? the beast asked far too innocently.

"Whoa," Jake said, hanging on to the dashboard while the tires screamed through the left turn.

"Sorry," she muttered, feeling her cheeks heat. She kept her mouth shut and her eyes on the road, hoping the breeze would cool her off before they got back to the resort.

"Wasn't that on the list?" Jake asked as they flashed past a sign.

"Wasn't *what* on the list?"

He motioned behind him. "Lahaina Second Friday. What is that anyway?"

"It's a big street party in Lahaina."

"Street party..." He considered.

She'd never been, but she'd heard about it.

Great music, Nina had said.

Great dancing, Tessa had added with a huge smile.

In other words, a terrible idea for a shifter in her horny state.

"Pretty good thing for a couple of honeymooners to do," Jake said.

She stared at him. Was he serious?

His eyes twinkled in the dim light. "We do have the car for twenty-four hours."

They did, but no. Not a good idea. Didn't he know that music and dancing could lead them down a long, tempting road?

The look on Jake's face said he didn't mind that one bit.

"I'm a mess. And you are too," she tried.

But her heart wasn't having that, and Jake wasn't either. He checked his watch. "We can grab a quick shower and come back. Plenty of time."

Ella pursed her lips. A good thing Jake wasn't a shifter — he would have sensed her eagerness all too well. "Maybe we ought to get back to checking out things at the resort. The reception is tomorrow, after all."

Jake tilted his head one way then the other. "It is one of the last things on Lily's list..." He left the words hanging as if it was all the same to him. But she could feel the hope rise within him — and damn it, within her too. An evening out with Jake would be much nicer than rushing back into a lie. And the day had been a good one, Gideon Goode aside.

Her fox nodded eagerly. *We definitely need to finish Lily's list.*

She looked at Jake, then at the dimming coastline, and finally into her heart. She wanted an evening out with him far too much, and damn it, this time, she just couldn't resist.

Just this once, she told her fox. *And just dancing.*

Just this once, the beast echoed immediately.

"I guess duty calls," she said. "I mean, finishing Lily's list and all."

Jake grinned. "Duty calls."

And so it was that instead of turning the car keys back in to the rental desk at the resort, they took turns rushing in and out of the shower before heading back to town. Parking was a nightmare, as Ella knew it would be, and the walk to the middle of town was long. But the stars shone overhead, and cheery people lined the streets, tourists and locals alike. The sound of a band drew them on, and she looked around.

"God, I haven't been here in ages."

Lahaina was a touristy place, and she had never really spent much time there, having grown up on the other side of the island. But it was surprisingly nice, even with the tourists, T-shirt stands, and kitschy souvenirs. The music drifting down the street from ahead pulled her on, and the timeless atmosphere of the town made her mind drift.

Just the two of us, her fox purred.

Just dancing, she reminded the beast. *Nothing else.*

Like Kai said, her fox reminded her. *It's our last night off before the reception. Gotta make it count.*

Which is exactly what she was afraid of doing. But, damn. The night was so warm, so full of possibility...

"Kind of nice," she said.

"Nice," Jake grunted, making her head turn.

His shoulders were bunched, his back stiff. Ella looked around and cursed herself. The noise, the crowds, the flashing lights had made Jake switch from eager to tense.

"Maybe we should forget it," she murmured.

"No." His voice was tight, his eyes all over the place.

Ella squeezed Jake's hand, trying to settle him down.

So, distract him, her fox tried.

"Lahaina was once a whaling port. There are lots of stories from the old days."

Jake nodded without saying a word.

So much for distracting him.

I meant with a kiss, her fox snipped.

She shook her head at her fox — no way — and tried again. "That's the Wo Hing house. It was kind of like a clubhouse for immigrants from China, way back when."

"Neat," Jake said in the same terse tone.

The music grew louder and the crowds thicker as they approached the center of town, and Ella paused, ready to turn around. But Jake plowed forward, as determined as a man heading into battle.

"We really don't have to," she said, following reluctantly.

"Yes, we do," he said, stomping on.

She let out a slow breath, wishing Jake didn't have so much to prove. So what if he was a little shy of crowds and noise? Lots of soldiers experienced that when they first came home. Hell, she had headed straight for the quietest corner of Arizona and all but disappeared into the desert for months. Everyone needed time to adjust.

"Wow," a woman said, and Ella followed her gaze.

"Wow," she whispered, stopping at the scene ahead.

The square behind the courthouse was festooned with hundreds of white lights, some hung over antique lampposts, others strung through the branches of the huge banyan tree.

"Honey, did you know this tree was planted in 1873?" the woman said to her partner, reading from a guidebook.

Ella nodded to herself. Yes, she knew. But somehow, she'd forgotten how beautiful it all was. Over the decades, the banyan had sent branches in every direction like dozens of explorers mapping the seven seas. Each branch shot down fresh roots before projecting outward in another long arch, creating a thick canopy overhead. Dozens of myna birds flicked in and out of the leaves, chirping as if they were part of the band, and kids ran around the thick tree trunks, playing hide-and-seek.

It was beautiful. Really beautiful. She might even have been tempted to sway to the music if Jake hadn't been so keyed up. He hesitated, and she started to turn around. "You know, let's go back to the hotel."

Jake sucked in a deep breath and straightened abruptly. His teeth were clenched and his jaw tight as he grabbed her hand and tugged her toward the center of the action.

"What are you doing?" she asked, jogging along beside him.

"Dealing with it," he barked.

Ella's eyes went wide when she realized what Jake meant. He was heading right to the middle of the crowd where couples danced in a tight knot of bodies. Where the lights shone brightest and the music blasted loudest. He staked out a spot, gritted his teeth, and swung her in a stiff pantomime of a dance.

"Do you mind?" he asked, as grimly resolute as a man heading into a war zone.

Mind a dance? No, she didn't mind. It wasn't so much a dance as a barely contained rage. But Jake was just as tenacious as he had been with that puzzle box, so all she could do was hang on. Cords of muscle stood out in etched rows along his arms, and his grip was so tight, it hurt. His breath came in ragged pants, and his eyes were squeezed tight.

"It's okay," Ella murmured, smoothing her hands over his shoulders. "Just me and my husband out for a nice night."

Jake's mouth curled into a brief smile before losing its humor again. But a teensy, tiny bit of his tension eased, so she rested her cheek on his shoulder and danced on.

"Oh," she mumbled, faking cheeriness. "This is the song we heard on the radio this afternoon."

Jake jerked his head up and down in a nod and lurched on.

She turned, putting her right cheek against his chest where she could hear his heart jackhammering away. So she closed her eyes and imagined a scene that would settle him down.

"You know, the ranch where I work puts on dances too," she whispered.

"Yeah?" Jake asked, not quite tuned in.

"Yeah," she said. "Twin Moon Ranch. They have good, old-fashioned barn dances under the stars. A little like this, but with a lot more space."

"That would be nice," Jake said in a flat tone.

She rocked her cheek across his shoulder, trying to communicate the peace and tranquility of that Arizona scene through her touch and thoughts. Jake might not be a shifter who could read her mind, but some of it might rub off.

She pictured fireflies flickering in the night. Couples dancing under colorful party lights. Other couples moved to where the music was fainter and danced under the stars, each pair dancing any way they liked. Lovers would whisper in each other's ears and smile. Kids would mimic them then collapse into giggles. Older folks watched from folding chairs set along the sides, sentimental smiles stretching on their faces as memories took them to times gone by.

Our mate would love it there, her fox whispered.

She nodded in spite of herself and whispered, "It's really nice. They have outdoor dances. No walls, just like this."

Jake nodded, and she did her best to imagine herself and Jake into that familiar scene on the edge of the endless Arizona plains. Plains that stretched on and on until they crashed into mountains that looked purple in the indigo-tinted night. So much space — enough to erase hurries, worries, and time. Enough for every person to find peace in his or her individual space.

Someone bumped her right elbow, snapping Ella back to Maui, and she glanced at Jake again. Was he doing any better?

It was hard to tell with his face turned away from hers, but his chest rose and fell in a steadier rhythm, and his tight muscles slowly unwound. She steered him away from the bandstand, maneuvering to a quieter spot where they could pretend to be alone. She spent a lot of time looking down at his chest, trying to figure out how that big and hard a range of muscle could create such a cozy place. And when she looked up, she smiled into his eyes.

"Nice dance," she whispered.

"Yeah. Great," he muttered, still not happy with himself.

"Maybe not yet, but it's getting there," she said, making him smile.

"You think so?"

His hands shifted slightly, and she nodded. "Better, for sure."

With one of Jake's big hands around her waist and the other at her shoulder, she felt warm. Protected. "I definitely think we're getting the hang of it."

"Not so sure," he mumbled.

Ella shrugged. "I'm no dancer, but it feels good to me." She jerked her chin upward, and his eyes followed. The branches of the mighty banyan tree formed an amphitheater, and with the party lights shining like so many stars, it seemed as if the outer reaches of the universe had hunched down for a closer look at what was going on. "How about you?"

He snuggled her a little closer. "Doesn't feel too bad."

She play-smacked his arm, trying to help him lighten up. "Not too bad?"

That coaxed out another smile, and he held her closer still. "This part is nice. Really nice."

"That's more like it, McBride," she muttered, pretending to be annoyed.

Jake grinned then closed his eyes again, and his next few steps were lighter, less forced. They danced through another song, not entirely aware of one ending and the next starting until they really were dancing, not just clinging to each other like a couple of shipwrecked sailors in a storm. The lights twinkled, and Ella's smile grew bigger.

"You're not too bad at this."

"Liar," he said, not the least annoyed.

"You are. Look."

She swung her right arm out, and Jake immediately pulled her into a turn. His eyes grew brighter, clearer. Freer of whatever dark place they had been. His hands slipped lower, pulling her hips closer to his. Closer still, until she became aware of something besides the need to settle Jake down.

Mate, her fox yowled. *Need my mate.*

A fire kindled inside her, hunger for more than a dance, and the way Jake's eyes shone at hers hinted he was thinking the same thing.

Which probably meant it was time to stop dancing before her fox got any bad ideas. But she didn't want to stop dancing. She didn't want to stop enjoying Jake. So she danced on, eyes closed, breathing in his woodsy scent. Feeling light years out of the military and like a normal civilian for a change. A person allowed to do anything she wanted. So why not enjoy a little dance? Heck, why not touch? Why not kiss?

She turned her head slowly, sniffing his neck, gradually turning toward his lips. She was vaguely aware of her fox sneaking closer and closer to the surface — but somehow, she no longer gave a damn.

"Ella," Jake started to say.

She shushed him. She was good with her body, and he was good with his. Both of them were better with actions than words.

So kiss him, her fox murmured.

Which was dangerous, but her resistance was worn down to nil.

Kiss him, an inner voice insisted, not giving her any time to think.

She turned a little more until his lips were right in front of hers. Full, shiny lips that weren't saying anything close to no. She rolled to the balls of her feet and slowly, carefully let her lips close over his.

Her fox groaned. *So good.*

Jake's hands tightened along the sides of her waist, and his thumbs stretched high, making her hungry for more.

She moved her lips, forming a silent, *I want this. I need this.*

I deserve this, her fox agreed.

Alarm bells went off throughout her mind, but she pulled a switch, silencing them. Damn it, she did deserve this.

Jake's lips eased open, inviting her in, and she deepened the kiss. Deeper and deeper, running her tongue over his. The outside world became a blur, and she went deliciously dizzy, clinging to him. Feeling lost — and found — in his embrace.

Chapter Ten

Jake closed his eyes during the drive back, savoring the taste of Ella's kiss. Not just the one under the banyan tree, but the other two as well. One came when she'd pulled him over on the walk back to the Jeep. A nice, long kiss that had him pressing her against the white picket fence of the Wo Hing museum — the place with all the paper lanterns glowing in the dark. The light coming from them was a soft shade of red — more the color of desire than the color of alarm. And before he knew it, his hands were sliding over Ella's perfect ass, and his brain was shutting down.

He'd barely managed to break it off and amble casually down the sidewalk again, keeping her nice and close. But when they got back to the pink Jeep, it was him ducking into another amazing kiss. A deep, hungry kiss that made his blood rush. Before he knew it, he was gliding a hand along her waist. Ella squeezed her body against his and whimpered, assuring him he wasn't the only one thinking of venturing past first base. But then a car beeped and a guy called out, laughing.

"Go for it, *brah*!"

He'd scowled at the guy's taillights. He didn't want to go for it with Ella. He wanted so much more.

"Cute little *wahine* you got there," the jerk's buddy called.

"Not little," Ella muttered. "Asshole. Him, I mean — not you."

Which made it that much easier to smile, pull apart, and get in the car.

So he'd gotten three kisses altogether, and any one of them could have gone down in the record books as the best kiss of all time. Part of his mind — the part wired directly to his cock

— wanted to fast-forward to all the other things he and Ella might get up to once they got back to their room...

Honeymoon suite, the bad-boy part of his mind emphasized with a wink.

... but if there was one thing he'd learned in the army, it was to relish good times while they lasted, because you never knew when the shit might hit the fan.

"Jake," Ella whispered as she turned the vehicle onto the main road.

He kept his eyes closed. Crap. Was she about to change her mind?

Her fingers closed gently around his, and she rested their clasped fists on his thigh. He took a deep breath, cementing that moment into his mind. Whatever Ella said next didn't matter. Only that feeling of completion did, no matter how fleeting it might be.

"Great kiss," she whispered.

He exhaled and tried not to grin like a fool. "Great kiss."

Their fingers remained intertwined the rest of the drive back, dancing around each other the way he wished their bodies could do, and they only broke apart briefly to get out of the car.

Jake nearly paused there, tempted to go for another kiss. But Ella seemed intent on reaching the privacy of their suite as soon as possible, and a guy didn't mess with a woman's momentum. Not at a time like that. So they walked — power-walked — hand in hand through the lobby and over to the elevator. A peek in the mirror made him grin. They really did have the honeymooner thing down pat.

The elevator binged cheerily as it rumbled upward, and still, Ella didn't say a word. Her hip bumped his side, though, and her hand slid along his back. He kept his arm looped over her shoulders, and the crackling energy between them intensified.

Honeymoon suite, his body cheered when they reached their floor.

He pushed the door open for Ella then followed her through. Housekeeping had been in, leaving them a bucket of ice and a bottle of champagne. Ella walked past it on her way to the balcony, fingering her silver chain.

"Nice night," she murmured in the moonlight.

Jake dipped his hand in the ice bucket as he passed, trying to cool down. "Nice night."

Ella was over by the railing, and he resisted the urge to step behind her and squeeze close. Or did she want him to do exactly that? But, no — that would make him come across as a rutting bull, so he stood beside her instead. Their bodies overlapped a tiny bit, his hip touching her left side, her hand closing over his as they took in the view. Boats bobbed on their moorings, moonbeams rippled over the sea. The sound of a piano drifted up from below, and phosphorescence glowed where waves rolled over the sand. But mostly, Jake sniffed Ella's scent and watched the breeze make her hair sway. Her body heat reached out toward him, inviting him closer. When he ran a hand lightly up her back, Ella's chest rose on a deep breath. Either she was getting ready to holler at him, or she liked the feel of that.

Her lips cracked open, and she sighed.

He lowered his hand, tracing her spine until he reached the swell of her ass. Still no holler, so he ran one finger up again.

"Jake," she whispered, letting her ass bump his hip.

He swept his hand downward, getting as far as her tailbone that time. His vision tunneled to just her back, leaving everything else a blur. They were six stories up, and the crest of the nearest palm tree did a slow hula. Jake had to give Maui that — the island screamed *sensual* no matter where you looked. Not that he needed that with Ella tilting her head, making her hair cascade to one side.

He bent to kiss the back of her neck. Slowly, gently. Ella reached around and cupped his cheek, pulling him closer. Closer...

He let his lips explore her soft flesh. The balcony was dotted with huge planters full of fragrant flowers, but Ella's scent was deeper than that of those flirty blossoms. Tougher, in a way, like a desert rose. He inhaled deeply, getting high on her.

"Mmm," Ella murmured, melting into his touch.

Jake closed his eyes and forced himself to go slowly. He touched her, exploring the topography of her body. Her stomach was flat and hard with muscle, her breasts soft and smooth.

"Nice," she whispered, covering his hand with hers and guiding it higher.

Both of them held their breath when his fingers found her nipple, where he traced a breathless circle. The soft button became a tight bead as he whisked his fingers around and around.

"Jake..." Ella arched slightly, and he opened his mouth, kissing her neck. She lifted and curled her arms backward, giving him more access until he had both hands on both breasts, kneading softly.

Yes... yes...

Ella didn't say anything, but her breath came in pants that coaxed him on.

Tell me what you want, and I will do it for you, he wanted to say. *Tell me how to make you feel good.*

She caught his right hand and guided it downward, skimming over her belly until he was cupping her mound. She slid sideways at the same time, pushing her ass against his groin, making his cock ache. And when she nudged his hand lower, he just about moaned.

Touch me. Touch me there, her unspoken command said.

The curve of her body guided his hand lower, and he rubbed until she was dancing under his hand. That made her dress rise an inch, and he fantasized about seeing more. Touching deeper. Licking her there. He kissed his way to her ear, where her scent was most intense.

She held back the whimpers and moans any other woman would mutter, because Ella didn't do those things. No showing emotion, no sign of weakness. But the movement of her body screamed lust and desire. Her ass ground against him, and her hands clutched at his shirt, pulling the tail out of his pants.

Want you so bad, her body cried when she turned in his arms and smothered him in a deep, lusty kiss.

Her chest expanded, and her nipples peaked so hard, he could feel them through the fabric of his shirt. Just as he thought Ella would wrap her legs around him and let her carry her inside, she broke off the kiss and gulped for air.

"Jake..."

Her chest heaved, and he gulped. This was it. The *stop* moment he'd been dreading all along.

"I want this as much as you do, but..."

"But what?" he asked, gripping her hips. If she ordered him to let go, he would, but hell — it would take a mental crowbar to do so.

"I can't do this. We can't do this."

He shook his head. If she had said, *I don't want this*, he'd have backed away and given her space. But her hands remained fisted in his shirt, her body pressed against his, her eyes full of hope. And eyes didn't lie. Especially not Ella's.

"What's stopping us?"

She shook her head and looked around desperately, hinting at some outside force, some pressure to resist. But what could that possibly be? They weren't in the army any more. No one would judge her for hooking up with him. So what was it?

"I'm dangerous for you," she said.

He snorted. Danger lay in overseas assignments and enemy domains. Danger lurked in the shadows, but not in the heart. How could this intense feeling of need be anything but good?

"Sometimes I think I feel most alive when I'm in danger," he muttered.

Ella's eyes darkened briefly before she broke into a weak smile. "I can relate to that."

He rolled his hands over her shoulders, aching to pull her nice and tight against his chest. He could count the number of people who understood him on one hand, and except for Ella, they were all men. And how many people understood Ella the way he did? Very few women, he'd bet, and even fewer men. Which made them perfect for each other, right?

The palm trees moved more quickly, urging him on.

"You know the only other time I feel alive?" he ventured.

She shook her head and waited.

"When I'm with you."

His pulse hammered in his veins, and his senses felt sharper than ever. Every deep breath felt like a cleansing of the soul and a step into the future.

Ella's mouth cracked open, but then she swallowed. "I mean it, Jake. I'm a danger to you. Trust me."

Trust me was Ella code for *Don't ask.* He tucked his chin until his forehead rested on hers, trying to puzzle that out. "You got a long-lost mafia uncle who'll put a hit on me?"

She shook her head, making his head move too. "No."

"So what is it? You want this, right?"

Her breath stuttered in and out. "I want this more than you know."

He doubted it. It wasn't just the ache in his cock that made him want her. His heart begged for her, too.

"I wish I could explain..." she murmured.

But she didn't explain, and he didn't press her, because pushing Ella only made her push back.

He lowered his head to her ear and nibbled at the lobe. "Come on, Kitt. You've lived dangerously before. You can do it for one more night."

Her hands wandered aimlessly over his chest, and the twitch of her fingers hinted at an inner battle.

"One more night..." she whispered.

He combed her hair back and kissed his way from her ear to the corner of her mouth. "Would be a shame not to put the honeymoon suite to good use."

She snorted then caught his chin with her hand. "What if I said yes to one night?"

Jake didn't say a word, sensing that question was aimed at herself. He let the slide of his hands answer in a different way, though.

I promise I'll make it really, really good.

"What if we agree to wild, raging sex?" Ella went on.

He dipped his chin in a nod that didn't begin to communicate the *please, please, please* bottled up inside.

"What if we both agreed to keep it to just one night?" she asked.

He doubted he could do that, but hell. He gave a quick nick of a nod. It was a hypothetical question, right?

Ella took a deep breath and looked down. At his chest? At the bulge in his pants? Was she trying to see through to his heart? He wished she could, because then she'd know he was for real.

"Promise me tonight is just tonight," she said, fisting his shirt.

He held his breath, not ready to promise that much. Luckily, she skipped right ahead to her next demand.

"Promise me we'll deal with tomorrow when we get there."

That, he could do. "I promise."

The words came out in a low, growly rumble, and Ella's eyes shone. They stood staring at each other for a full ten seconds before her lips twitched. And somehow, like a secret signal, that set everything off.

Their lips crushed together, their bodies meshed. Ella tasted him deeply, exploring his mouth while he kneaded her perfect ass. It was just like their first night together, all that time ago. The animal intensity, the raw desire. But it was totally different, too, because instead of divesting her of camo fatigues, all he had to deal with was that dress.

"Hang on," he murmured, hitching her hips higher.

She split her legs around his waist and let him carry her inside. She didn't release his mouth, though, and they ended up bumping into the walls and the couch a couple of times. But Ella was tough — and hungry — and didn't mind one bit. The second they were in the bedroom, she dropped her feet to the floor and yanked at his shirt.

"Gotta lose this, soldier."

"Yes, ma'am," he said, though she was the one doing most of the work. And quick work too. She got his belt loose and his pants off, then palmed his cock hard.

Oh, yes, her wide eyes said when she shoved his boxers down, letting him spring free.

Jake could have gone down over her right there on the floor, but she was still dressed.

"Nuh-uh," he murmured, holding her hands back before she pulled the dress over her head. "I'm doing that."

Ella didn't take orders well, but she seemed okay with that one. "Be my guest, McBride."

He turned her so her back was up against his chest, facing the floor-to-ceiling mirror along the long side of the bed.

"Aw, no fun," she protested when he pulled her hands clear of his cock. He had to if he was going to do anything but tear that dress off with his teeth.

"Oh, it'll be fun," he rumbled, nodding to the mirror. "Watch."

Ella stuck her chin up in defiance, but her eyes sparkled with lust. The mirror showed her — fully dressed, if not for long — plus him, buck-naked but sheltered behind her so his monster erection didn't show, thank God. Behind them in the reflection they could see the rest of the suite and all the way out to the rippling shadows of the night.

He slid his hands up and down her body, teasing her by bouncing too quickly over her breasts. Then he collected her hair in one hand and revealed the clasp at the back.

"You know what?" he murmured while he figured out how to undo the damn thing.

"What?"

"Getting you out of a dress is even better than getting you out of fatigues."

She chuckled and tapped her foot impatiently. "It's slower, though."

"Slow?" He pulled the dress over her shoulders and tossed it aside. But damn it, underneath that, she wore a thin, silky thing. Another layer?

She chuckled. "Told you. Slow."

"Slow can be good," he said, running his hands over her tattoos. Someday, he'd ask her about the patterns. But right now. . .

"How can slow be g— Oh!" she cried out as he tweaked her nipple through the silk. Her eyes glassed over as she watched in the mirror.

"See? Good," he whispered. His cock surged against her, echoing the point.

The undergarment was the smoothest, silkiest thing he had ever touched, a sea of shining ivory except where the points of her nipples stood out. He gathered the fine silk in his hands, working it just high enough to reach her panties and push them down. Ella helped with a wiggle of her ass that he didn't dare comment on. Jesus — he would never utter a word to any of the guys at Koa Point, but man, had they misjudged Ella if all they saw was her tomboy side. Under all that was a sensual woman with moves that could blow a man's mind.

A rumble of pleasure built in his throat as he thought that over. No one got to see that side of Ella. No one but him.

He refocused in the mirror, suddenly hungry to see more. The panties were gone, which meant the second he got the slip off her...

She raised her arms on cue, and wow, *slip* was the word. One quick movement and it wafted over her head then fluttered to the floor.

She undid her bra and tossed it aside, and Jake couldn't help but stare. Those pert, round breasts. Her smooth belly. The inviting thatch of curls at the apex of her legs.

Ella laughed and curled her arms backward around him. "Not your first rodeo, cowboy."

No, it wasn't, but wow. The one night they had shared had been in the back of a supply tent. No lights, no mirror, and definitely no paintings of roses to set the honeymoon mood. He cupped her breasts and flicked his thumbs over her nipples, making her arch.

"Anyone ever tell you how beautiful you are?"

He was pretty sure she would have socked him if he ever said as much before, but he couldn't help it.

"Anyone ever tell you— Oh!" she broke off the smart-aleck response and arched harder when he repeated the movement. Then he reached down and touched her between the legs, making her moan.

Jake could have spent an hour watching the mysteries of Ella unfold. Watching her surrender to his touch and dance under his hands. But at some point, her eyes flashed, and some switch in him flipped too. His careful touches became desperate gropes, and a blink of an eye later, they were on the floor.

"I can't believe we have an entire honeymoon suite, and we're doing it on the rug," Ella chuckled as he rooted around in the bedside drawer for a condom.

He ripped the packet open with his teeth and kneeled over her. "We can save those nice silk sheets for next time." Maybe then he'd be able to take it slow, because this round was going to be anything but.

"Next time," Ella said, spreading her legs wide. Casually, comfortably, like they did this every night. "I like the sound of that."

He rolled the condom over his straining cock then he lowered himself to his elbows and looked down. God, that was hot, seeing her hips jut up, eager to connect.

"Nice view," Ella murmured, angling his cock toward her core.

He glanced up and found her head turned to the side, watching them in the mirror.

"Never knew you had a voyeuristic side, Kitt."

"Lots of things you don't know about me, McBride."

When he pinned her hands over her head and squeezed them in a question, her eyes flashed.

Yes, they said. *I want you. Hard. Fast. Deep.*

He thrust forward, sliding inside her with one hard push.

Ella moaned and arched into him, digging her nails into his hands. "Again," she panted a second later. "Do that again."

He withdrew until just the tip of his cock was in contact with her entrance and then plunged in, making her cry out.

"Jake... again... "

Even as her body stretched to accommodate him, the squeeze on his cock remained painfully, perfectly tight. She met every one of his thrusts with a quick flex of her inner muscles, making him groan out loud. He peeked in the mirror too, and though it was satisfying to see his body piston against hers, nothing beat the sight of Ella coming totally undone. Her hair fanned out around her head. Her breasts were soft pillows that glistened with beads of sweat. Her mouth opened and closed on a dozen whispered urgings no one would ever hear but him.

"So good... Oh, Jake... More..."

He gave her everything he had, thrusting hard, pausing only to hitch her leg higher against his side and power forward once more. The thrusts became a steady rhythm that grew until he faltered, and with one last push—

Jake threw his head back as he exploded inside her.

Ella shuddered as she came with a cry that stretched on and on, while Jake closed his eyes to relish the sweet burn. Then her body relaxed, and her hands fluttered over his back. Jake dropped to her chest, pinning her with his weight, unable to move. Ella wrapped her arms and legs around him and sighed while he panted against her skin in one of those oxygen-debt moments that only came after the hardest, longest runs. Then slowly, reluctantly, they both rolled to one side.

Damn it. He had to get rid of that condom, but he never wanted to leave her arms. Ella groaned when he hurried to the bathroom to dispose of it, then giggled.

"What?" he asked, memorizing the view before he came back down over her. Ella, very naked and very satisfied, her legs still spread, saving that space for him.

He nestled right into position and let her nuzzle him. That, he remembered too. It seemed like the last time they'd spent the night together, she had devoted every second of recovery time to nuzzling him. Which wasn't as good as sex, but pretty damn close in a cozy, chicken-soup-for-the-soul kind of way.

She giggled and murmured into his shoulder. "You know what Kai said?"

He squinted at her. What the hell did Kai have to do with mind-blowing sex with the most amazing woman in the world?

"He said to take the night off and make it count." She chuckled, drawing her leg higher along his side. "So I guess we ought to make the most of it."

"Yes, ma'am," Jake breathed.

Chapter Eleven

And they did make the most of the night, Ella decided as she lounged naked on the couch a few hours later. Shatteringly good sex on the floor had led to the sweetest, sultriest sex she'd ever had in bed — and yes, the silk sheets were nice too, especially when she'd straddled Jake and took in the view of him, glassy-eyed, satisfied, and balls deep in her, with his arms swimming over all that silk.

By the time they called for room service afterward, she'd been so into her naked-and-sensual groove that she nearly answered the door in her birthday suit.

"Oops," she said, letting Jake cinch up a bathrobe — hers, not his — and answer the door instead. When he wheeled the trolley into the living room, she couldn't help ruffling the fluffy collar of the robe. "I think you're getting in touch with your feminine side."

Jake's eyes roved over her body. His eyes said, *You're the one getting in touch with your feminine side.*

Well, okay. Maybe she was. Cute outfits and glittery heels might not be her thing, but frolicking naked with her stud of a man was definitely bringing out her girly side. Who knew flirting could be such fun? She'd also discovered the advantage of letting her hair down, because the swing and bounce seemed to fascinate Jake. His eyes would rove from there to her shoulders to her breasts, where they rested for a breathless minute before he jerked them away.

Good old Jake. Good manners. No trace of sexist pig. And Jesus, the man was a titan in bed. Which, of course, she knew, because it wasn't their first time together. But in another sense, it felt like the first time — first time outside military rules of engagement and on their own terms.

Of course, that didn't solve the crux of the shifter-human issue she was increasingly tempted to explain, but she was determined to put all that aside for the night.

"Not too chilly?" Jake asked, stroking her leg absently.

They both sat sideways on the couch, him at one end, her at the other, with their legs intertwined in the middle. Jake motioned over his shoulder toward the wide-open sliding doors. The flower-print curtains danced in the breeze, as if to say, *Don't you want to come out here again?*

She grinned, because she and Jake had followed up dinner with a good hour on the balcony, and only a fraction of that time had been spent looking at the view. She'd slid down to her knees and satisfied the burning desire to taste him. And man, had it been fun to have Jake at her mercy for a change. She'd peeked up from time to time, watching him grip the handrail and tip his head back in ecstasy. He was a hell of a lot better at holding back sounds than she was, but she'd still gotten a few throaty groans out of him, especially when he came.

She took another swing of champagne and smacked her lips. Yeah, that had been good. She might have to try it again soon.

"Chilly? No, I'm fine," she said, drawing her heel along his leg. She let her eyes follow the motion, taking in the lines of muscle along his thighs before focusing on his stomach. Lots of guys in the military had good abs, but Jake...

He looked up, catching her peeking — again — and grinned.

"Definitely not chilly?" His eyes danced with mischief.

Ella tried to figure out which answer would get her to sex faster and settled on letting her knees drop apart another inch, making Jake's eyes dip then bounce back to her face. She hadn't shifted for days, making her wild and reckless.

"You feeling the need to heat me up or cool me down?" she asked, channeling her inner Marilyn Monroe.

Jake pushed aside the coffee table and kneeled beside her. "Lie back," he murmured, reaching behind him.

She arched an eyebrow, because a girl didn't just do what a guy said.

Except when he has masterful hands and a really good tongue, her inner fox hummed.

Okay, maybe she would do as she was told, just this once. She wiggled farther down the couch and lay back, watching him. Goose bumps rose along her skin out of sheer anticipation. They had already compared scars and tickled each other's toes. "What form of torture do you have for me next?"

"Torture, huh? Close your eyes."

She considered for a second, then did as he said. "Okay, but no handcuffs, McBride. No blindfolds. No tying me up."

He chuckled. "Not my kind of thing, unless you want to try it sometime."

Sometime. Her inner fox sighed. She liked the *we have years ahead of us* sound of that.

"Just lie still," Jake murmured.

She sniffed, catching the rich scent of the hyacinths in a vase on the table and a heady whiff of Jake's fresh, leather-and-bergamot scent. He stirred something, and she heard a clink. Next came a tiny drip — and another — drops of water falling quietly against the floor. When Jake touched her belly with the flat of his callused hand, she held her breath, waiting. He circled her skin with one bold finger, and then—

"Oh!" she squeaked, arching up at a sudden burst of cold.

"And I thought you were tough, Kitt," he teased, moving away.

She nearly peeked — was that an ice cube? — but he covered her eyes. "Are you ready or not?"

She settled back, telling her muscles to unwind. "Ready. If you must."

"Oh, I must."

Which was a damn good thing, because now that she had an inkling of what he was up to, she desperately wanted more. It was amazing what an ice cube against bare skin could do. Of course, Jake could probably scrape dirty dishes across her body and make her howl with pleasure, she was so keyed up.

Want my mate, her fox yowled. *Now.*

It seemed the more she got of Jake, the more she craved. Which fit what she had heard — that lust intensified between destined mates until they bonded with a bite. And even afterward, the sex drive never waned, remaining a satisfying ritual rebonding of souls for life.

In which case, she was a goner. Worse, Jake would be a goner.

Tomorrow, her fox whispered. *We'll find a solution tomorrow. Don't ruin tonight with those things.*

The ice cube touched down on her belly again, and she yelped.

"You said you weren't chilly." Jake tsked.

"I'm not," she insisted, letting her legs flop open another inch.

"Then what's with the goose bumps?"

She grinned. "Those aren't from cold. In fact, I'm feeling rather hot."

"Good," he murmured in a sinfully sinister way.

Jake shifted, and the ice cube skated higher along her centerline. She tensed and arched as it moved, waking up the few remaining nerve endings that hadn't yet thrummed with need.

"Good," she whispered as he circled the ice cube around her breast. "Oh!"

She couldn't help wiggling and squeaking as he moved it around one breast, then the other. Her nipples peaked so hard, they ached, and she was tempted to touch herself. But there was no need as it turned out, because Jake leaned over her a second later, pulling her nipple between his lips.

Her whole body surged at the sensation. The cold bump of the ice cube on one nipple, the heat of Jake's mouth on the other. Then he switched, kissing her far breast while moving the ice cube to the near side. She writhed, unable to keep still yet not daring to move away. She threw one arm over her head, plumping out her breast for him, and ran the other hand through his hair, pressing his head closer.

"So good," she mumbled, closing her eyes.

"Yeah?" he said in a deep voice that vibrated through her chest.

Hell yeah, she nearly replied.

"Then how about this?" He nudged her knees wider, took hold of her hand, and guided it down.

Ella's eyes snapped open. He wanted her to touch herself?

"No peeking," he said, catching her at it.

She shut her eyes, obeying without thinking because she was that deep under his spell.

"You're peeking," she pointed out, trying to strike a casual tone as his big hand covered hers and started circling around.

"Bet your ass, I am. Now, hush," he said. "And breathe."

She didn't even realize she'd been holding her breath until then, because it was all so surreal. Touching herself wasn't anything new — not with the way she'd pined for Jake over the past too-many months — but she'd never done it with anyone looking on.

"Keep going," he whispered.

He swung away for a new ice cube then got back to work on her breasts, and she started stroking herself more boldly, imagining it was him. She ran her fingers through her folds, feeling the slickness build. Then she slipped a finger deeper and rolled it around.

"Good," Jake murmured, sucking on her breast.

Electrifying was more like it. She oohed and aahed with every roll of Jake's lips, every push of her fingers. Then she started bucking against an invisible saddle, panting harder and harder.

"Jake," she groaned.

"Don't stop," he said, almost as breathless as her.

She opened her eyes — breaking the rules, but okay — and gawked. Was that really her, being ravished by that hulk of a man? And was she really touching herself that hard and deep?

Yes, her fox groaned, echoing her ecstasy. *Yes.*

The wet remnants of an ice cube wobbled between her breasts, and her skin glistened. She switched to her right hand, leaving her leg to grope blindly around until it bumped Jake's long, hard, cock. With fingers slick from her own body, she started stroking him.

"Come to me," she mumbled as a roaring sound built in her ears.

Jake's muscles were coils of steel, his voice tight. "Just a second."

It felt so good, she was tempted to bring herself over the edge. But she could jack off on her own anytime she wanted. There was no way she was coming without Jake buried deep inside.

"Hell of a way to spend our honeymoon," she joked.

Jake gave her a tight grin. "Three seconds longer."

She tipped her head back and rocked harder. Three seconds, she could do.

"Three...two..." Jake accented the countdown with alternating nips and licks. "One."

He pulled away and reached for a condom, bumping the champagne bucket in his haste. Ice cascaded across the floor and glittered like so many diamonds. "Oops."

"Never mind. Get over here, soldier."

The couch was in the middle of the lounge, and she tossed the pillows aside to make room for Jake. A second later, he climbed over her and paused long enough for a kiss she reared into. When she flopped back with a hungry, *show me your stuff* nod, he went all serious. A second later, he plunged deep, deep inside.

Ella moaned openly, not bothering to hide it any more. The man made her feel alive. Beautiful. Deserving of someone like him. So, yes. She'd howl as much as she pleased, letting him know just how good he made her feel.

"Yes," she panted as he thrust into her again and again.

Yes, her fox cried, eyeing his neck, fantasizing about a mating bite.

Ella squeezed her eyes shut. Jake was doing it again — driving her wild, pushing her animal side to the forefront. And for the first time ever, she could imagine what her mother must have felt. The instinctive urge to mate, the *I can't live without him* recklessness that could drive a woman — and a willing man — over the edge. But death lurked on the other side of that invisible line, just like the shades of night that loomed where the lights of their suite faded away.

With a determined huff, Ella shoved all those thoughts to the back of her mind. Tonight was tonight, and she was going to make it count, no matter what came.

Jake rose to his knees, hauled her hips right off the couch, and pumped into her again. All the blood rushed to her head, making her dizzy with desire.

"Three... two..." he grunted, giving her another countdown.

On *one*, she squeezed over his cock and cried out at the searing heat inside.

Jake threw his head back and bared his teeth like the animal she wished he could become. They both shuddered, moaned, and eventually collapsed to the couch, where she stroked his bare back again and again.

"Jake," she whispered into the dark, wishing she could add, *My mate.*

Mate, her fox echoed sadly. *My mate.*

Chapter Twelve

Jake's usual morning routine involved waking up, waiting for the sun to rise while cursing the fact that he hadn't slept well, and thinking over the day ahead. But when he woke in the honeymoon suite, it wasn't a usual morning in any way. The sun was already illuminating the east side of the balcony. He'd slept like a rock, and all he could think of was a dream come true. A night with Ella. Talking. Touching. Lying in silence and staring into her eyes. He'd gotten to do all that, plus the bonus of holding her close while they slept.

The shower was running, and wow — the clock said 7:30 a.m. His body was still warm from where she'd curled against him, his arm still stuck out to shelter her. Somehow, Ella had slipped out of that protective cave without waking him, but if there were anyone who could pull that off, it would be her.

The door to the bathroom popped open, and she came out in the cloud of steam.

"Good morning," she whispered, lighting up upon seeing him.

Even better, she practically glowed throughout the five steps to the couch and bent over him with a kiss. She had one towel wrapped around her hair and another around her body, though the latter drooped the second she sat next to him. And that kiss... Soft. Practiced. Full of unspoken words.

"Good morning." He inhaled her fresh, shampoo scent and ran a hand over her bare shoulder.

Wow, were her eyes shiny. And man, her cheeks as well. Radiant, you might even say. He was pretty sure he was wearing a goofy grin and glowing too.

"I guess we'd better get going," she said, looking like she'd rather join him there on the couch. "Big day ahead."

"Big day," he echoed, still so blown away that words felt clunky on his tongue.

Ella's sunny expression sobered a moment later, and she took him by both hands. "Listen, Jake. I need to tell you something."

He sat up, nodding. It sounded kind of ominous, but then again, she hadn't said *We need to talk* which could be code for *It was a great night, but this will never work.*

She took a deep breath but pursed her lips, not quite ready to let the cat out of the bag. He rubbed his fingers over her arm, waiting.

"You know what I said last night?" she asked at last.

His mind raced from *I'm dangerous for you* to *I want this more than you know* and on to *Oh, Jake... more...* There was also the dreaded, *What if we keep it just to one night?* So, which did she mean?

"Uh, the part about no handcuffs, no blindfolds, no tying you up?" he joked.

She broke into a smile and swatted his arm. "Not that part, McBride."

"Kind of figured," he murmured, holding his breath as she grew serious again.

"The part about how I can't have you."

He nodded ever so slightly, trying to pull together a convincing speech in his mind. Something like, *I don't buy that. You know all those times you get a feeling you can't really explain, but you know you'd better listen to it, or else? That's this. That's us. We should be together. We have to be together.*

So few people had the blazing chemistry he and Ella did — at least, no one he'd ever met — and he thought of all the men he'd seen die early, before they could get around to the really important things. Before they could answer their sweetheart's letters or get around to saying what needed to be said. And even worse, the dying last words spoken to a comrade rather than a lover. *Tell her I love her. Tell her...*

He swallowed hard and moved his lips, hoping to get that out. There was a time to give a woman her space and a time to talk straight up. To fight for what he believed in.

But Ella beat him to it by pulling him into a huge hug and burying her face in his shoulder. "I want to tell you, but I don't know how."

He squeezed her close then slowly pulled back to look into her eyes. "So let me tell you. We fought for so many things, you and me. We can fight for us too."

Her eyes shone, hopeful yet sad. "What if it kills you, Jake? What if..."

That wasn't exactly what he'd been expecting. "A lot of things might have killed me. But they didn't, so I have to make my chance count." He took a deep breath, because it was time to tell her the one thing he'd never shared with anyone. "A year ago in March, about a month after I saw you—"

It had actually been thirty-two days and five hours after he'd seen her for the last time, but he left that part out.

"—we were heading out to protect a convoy way out somewhere near Kamdesh. Our Humvee was supposed to be second in line. Second, okay? But there was a delay with another unit, and we got switched to the front. No big deal, right?"

Ella's eyes took on an *oh, shit* look as he went on.

"The other guys caught up and took our original spot, and an hour later..." He stopped to scrub the heel of his hand over his thigh. "We hit an ambush. Well, our vehicle missed the mines. But that second vehicle hit them and got blasted to bits. The one that was supposed to be us."

His nose wrinkled, and he winced at the echo of that blast. For a while, he had just felt hollow, but then Manny had initiated that talk. That *We need to make our second chance count* talk.

Ella gripped his hand but didn't say a word.

"We had a long, hard look at ourselves after that. Each of us tried to figure out what really counted. And we promised each other that we'd make our second chance count when we left the service. So Manny made a dream come true by setting up an auto body shop. Junger took off to climb a couple of mountains..."

Ella chuckled faintly. Fondly. Junger had been one of those larger-than-life guys everybody liked. Jake wondered if Ella knew he was dead — and if Hoover's crazy theory was right.

Someone is taking us out, one by one.

He shook off the edgy feeling and went on. "Chalsmith vowed to patch things up with his ex and petition for more time with his kids. Hoover wanted to report for his local newspaper..." He left out the *and became a paranoid maniac* part. "...and I decided to travel to all fifty states."

She smiled. "Starting with Hawaii?"

He shook his head. "No. Yes. I mean..." His mouth was dry as hell, so the rest came out gritty, but at least he got it out. "That's what I said. But what I really wanted was to come after you." Then he stammered because, shit, that didn't sound right at all. "I mean, to find you. I mean..."

Crap. He would have done better banging his head against a wall a few times.

Ella's mouth swung open. "You wanted to find me?"

"I wanted to, but I didn't want to either. Well, I didn't want to admit as much. I guess I was worried you might prefer the guy you met back then."

She shook her head immediately and kissed his knuckles. "You're the same guy. Well, no. Not exactly. But I think I like this guy even more."

His heart thumped so hard, it hurt.

Her eyes shone. Almost glowed, in fact. "That's why I don't want to hurt you, Jake."

"So, talk to me. Tell me what's wrong. Let's figure something out."

Her eyes flickered. "It's hard to explain. Hard to understand too. A little scary, even."

What the hell could it possibly be? Jake squeezed her hands. "The only thing that scares me is regret."

Ella's throat bobbed in a heavy swallow. Then she took a deep breath and spoke. "It's like this. It's who we are. You're a man, and I'm— Damn it." She broke off as the phone rang.

Her phone, not the hotel phone, and the only people who called her private line were the men of her unit.

Jake eased back, forcing himself to give Ella space when what he really wanted was to throw the phone out the window, lock the door, and keep her to himself for the rest of the day until they finally got everything out in the open. Better yet, the rest of the week. Possibly even for the rest of his life.

"Yes?" She listened then sat straighter. "Got it. Start our patrols at eight." Another second ticked by as Ella listened, then she nodded. "Roger."

It wasn't a long call, but while she was talking, the outside world crept back into their private world. Jake could feel it practically slithering under the door like a dark mist. His eyes strayed to the clock, just as Ella's did. Twenty to eight.

The brightness went out of her eyes as she punched the phone off. "That was Kai. He wants us to start earlier today."

Jake forced himself not to frown. Changing plans was a way of life in the military. But Kai's timing could not have been worse.

"I guess we have to get going," he sighed, wishing he could carve another five minutes out of the time they'd had right before that call.

Ella opened her mouth, closed it, and finally nodded. "I guess so." Her hand tightened around his. "But we will talk. Once we get this reception out of the way and everything settles down. I promise I'll explain."

Then she leaned in for a kiss. A long, lingering, wistful one that gave him all the promise he needed.

She rose slowly, faking a light tone. "I already beat you to the first shower."

Jake forced himself out of bed. *Back to work, soldier. No more messing around.* "I guess I'm next, then."

And just like that, they both slipped back into work mode. Which meant showering military style – quickly, efficiently — and getting dressed. Ella in a blue dress that complemented the color of her eyes, him in slacks and a polo shirt so he wouldn't look out of place. Being undercover, they wouldn't be attending the reception, just keeping an eye on the grounds.

Silas had extra security coming in for the reception, but Jake and Ella were the ones who'd developed a sense of what fit in and what didn't.

Within fifteen minutes, they were both ready to go. When they stepped out of the room, their hands automatically clasped as they'd done all week. But it was different in a hundred invisible ways. His pulse skipped in hope, and his body tingled all over, remembering everything they'd done. Her hand fit perfectly in his, and her grip was the kind that said *Mine*.

Jake hid a smile and squeezed her hand the same way. *Mine.*

Silas and Cassandra's reception was scheduled to take place in the ballroom of the resort, and though it wasn't for another few hours, things were already bustling when Jake and Ella reached the ground floor. The caterers were unloading, staff was setting up tables, and florists scurrying around, setting up bouquets.

"Wow. Looks like a hell of a reception," Ella said loudly.

Jake kissed her hand. "Nothing beats ours."

She glowed — literally — and Jake smiled. Technically, he and she were married. They may not have had a reception, but somehow, it seemed like they had. Like they'd had their ceremony under the banyan tree the previous evening, and the reception had taken place on their balcony under all the twinkling stars.

After breakfast — him facing one way, keeping an eye on the lobby doors, and Ella facing the other, watching the caterers come and go — they set out for a stroll, keeping up appearances as the happy couple they were. Then Ella held up her camera and a book on Hawaiian flowers and spoke loud enough for any passerby to hear. "I think I'd like to try out some new camera settings. Okay with you, honey?"

Taking pictures was code for walking the perimeter. Jake would do the same from a different angle. So they went their separate ways, each covering a different part of the resort grounds. Afterward, Ella staked out the action from a lounge chair at poolside while Jake headed to the golf center to pick up some gear. There was a putting green outside the windows of the ballroom — the perfect place for him to keep an eye on things. He couldn't golf for his life, but he didn't mind the heft of the golf club in his hand. A weapon, if he needed it to be. But there wasn't any unusual activity, just business as usual, or at least to the extent that a major social event allowed.

"Ready for a drink, honey?" he said, meeting Ella at eleven.

"A drink sounds great. At the teahouse?"

The teahouse overlooked the polo grounds, and they'd already staked it out as a prime observation spot. Jake sat at an angle that allowed him a good, long look at any vehicle coming down the resort drive, while Ella kept her eye on the beach side, their weakest flank. Eventually, they took another walk, checking the perimeter yet again. When they returned from that loop of the grounds, hand in hand, Kai came ambling the other way. They didn't greet each other openly, but Jake subtly steered Ella to a bench where he paused to tie his shoelace. Kai pretended to stop for a phone call, acting exactly as if he were talking to someone on the other end of the line instead of murmuring to them.

"All clear?"

Ella nodded ever so slightly without turning to look. "All clear. Did you find anything on Goode?"

Kai's features grew hard. "No, but we're on it. Believe me, we're on it."

Jake sure hoped so. Few men made him as uneasy as Goode had done.

"Everything quiet last night?" Kai murmured.

Jake kept his eyes firmly on the shoelace. *Quiet* may not have been the best word, but he wasn't going to give anything away.

"Yep," Ella murmured, keeping a perfectly straight face.

Jake straightened and gave Kai a tiny nod of parting. But just as they were moving past each other, Kai's nostrils flared, and his head snapped around.

Oh, shit. Jake felt his heart sink as Kai stared in surprise.

"Don't you two look positively radiant this morning. Taking the cover story pretty seriously, huh?" Kai teased.

Jake had never come that close to socking a man he respected. Ella, to her credit, didn't blush or roll her eyes. She just smiled sweetly, still playing her role – though her right fist clenched hard. Kai must have seen it because he laughed and stepped away.

"As Georgia Mae would say, *Well, well.* Enjoy the rest of your honeymoon, kids. Just make sure you keep an eye out for bad guys."

Chapter Thirteen

Jake took Ella's elbow and walked away, his stomach churning. Ella had already tensed up, and he could sense her inhibitions coming back. The worry of losing status as one of the guys. Of being judged.

"Hey," he whispered. "It's none of Kai's business."

Her eyes flicked downward, and she veered off for the lobby, motioning vaguely. "I think I'll stop by our room for a second."

He kicked the dirt, watching her go. That was code for taking a short break, as Silas had insisted they do to remain as alert as possible while on the job, but still. Ella was running away from him, and it hurt to see her go.

He headed back to the lobby and picked up a newspaper, quietly observing the crowd in the ballroom grow. There was nothing out of the ordinary, though.

"Mr. Mayor. Mrs. Tang," someone called.

A flock of older ladies from some kind of animal rights charity group appeared too, chattering away in excitement.

"I'm so delighted they're getting married," one chirped.

The woman next to her beamed. "The first time I saw them together, I knew."

Jake chewed that one over. The first time he'd seen Ella, he had known too. He'd had a feeling of *forever*, of a perfect fit. Fool that he was, he'd denied it back then, but he wouldn't make that mistake again.

Boone and Nina arrived next, with Boone in one of his rare, *I'm actually wearing a suit and tie* moments, drawing the appreciative eye of the ladies. Nina looked absolutely radiant – or was the pink in her cheeks a little too red? Boone and the older ladies fussed over her as she lowered herself into a chair and fanned her face.

"I'm fine. I'm fine. No problem."

"I swear those babies are ready to pop any minute," one of the older ladies whispered to another.

God, Jake hoped not.

The hubbub grew as guests arrived in a steady stream. Most of the local ladies wore colorful island dresses with white flowers tucked behind one ear. Others came dressed for a red-carpet event in Hollywood, and the men were all in crisp suits and ties. Jake scanned every face for someone who might have a forced, *I swear, I'm not up to anything* look. Because who knew? He could imagine a woman jealous of Cassandra for picking up Maui's most eligible bachelor or a man out for revenge for something in Silas's past.

The thought made every muscle in Jake's body tense as Hoover's words echoed through his mind. *I'm telling you, man. Someone is taking us out, one by one.*

That shouldn't affect Silas's reception, but suddenly, Jake wasn't so sure. What if someone really was after his unit — and what if that person was stalking him here in Maui? That doubled the potential risk of this public event. Jake studied the crowd, the staff, and the premises for any telltale detail, any giveaway sign. But there was nothing suspicious, just a jovial crowd and the sound of a string quartet starting up. Not a hint of that *being watched* feeling he imagined Manny, Chalsmith, or Junger must have felt seconds before their lives were cut short. The hair-standing-up-on-the-back-of-his-neck feeling he'd had before the car had nearly run him down. On the contrary, the palm trees lining the nearby beach swayed and danced, miming, *This is Maui. A little corner of paradise. Relax.*

No, he would not relax. Could not. He was on the job.

So he moved to a better vantage point and continued mentally dividing the crowd into sections, dissecting each for any hint of trouble. Ella returned from her break but immediately detoured to the resort's front veranda to watch from there.

"Anything?" Kai murmured as he walked by.

Jake gave a curt shake of the head. Nothing. Ella was avoiding him, which sucked. But as far as the reception went, everything checked out — so far. Still, it was increasingly difficult to keep an overview of things. Between a pregnant woman, some pretty decently cleaned-up guys, and the thrill of a wedding, the guests grew more and more excited. By the time Silas and Cassandra showed up in a Rolls-Royce driven by Hunter, there were a dozen reporters waiting on the resort steps, and even Jake had to gawk at the scene. If someone had asked him back when he first met Silas whether the fatigue-clad, battle-hardened commander had what it took to become an *I'm so in love, there are stars in my eyes* almost-newlywed, Jake would have laughed. But there was Silas, all spiffed up in a tux, with eyes only for his bride-to-be. Cassandra looked great and managed being in the limelight admirably well. She stopped to smile and talk – really talk – to each guest eager to clasp her hand.

Once the couple of the hour was inside the ballroom, Jake had a good look around and moved to a stool in the restaurant bar, where he could overhear the action and peek through the open ballroom doors. A spoon clinked on a glass, and the chatter died down.

"Well, I think it's time to begin," Silas murmured, quieting the last voices with his deep baritone.

Ella walked up and slipped into a seat beside Jake, tilting her head and listening, too.

"Someone said they were surprised to see me engaged," Silas started. "Believe me when I say I'm more surprised than anyone else."

Jake smiled faintly as chuckles rippled through the room.

"Some surprises, well — they're not so good," Silas went on.

Jake's cheek twitched as he thought about the day of the ambush.

"But some surprises are good ones. Really good," Silas said. "The kind that make you wonder why fate decided to give so much to one man."

Yeah, Jake knew that feeling too. Meeting Ella had been like that — and last night, too. He glanced over, but her eyes were firmly on the doors.

Silas continued, but a phone rang in the reception area, and a sports car hummed by outside, so Jake only caught some parts.

"Love. . ."

". . . duties that sometimes seem crushing. . ."

Ella nodded as if she knew exactly what Silas meant.

A caterer came by with a rattly trolley of dishes, drowning out most of the next part of Silas's speech.

". . . But when destiny talks, it's best to listen, and I learned that no man is immune. . ."

A man in the lobby started chattering on his phone, and whatever Silas said next was lost. But Hunter, who was standing by the ballroom doors, wore a goofy, sentimental look. The same look Boone had as he kissed Nina. They were just within Jake's line of sight at the side of the ballroom, and the mirrors gave him a glimpse of Kai reaching for Tessa's hand.

"Destiny," Ella whispered. Her eyes locked on Jake's.

Destiny, he nearly echoed. Was there really such a thing?

A moment later, Ella blinked and tensed again, fingering the silver necklace she wore.

"My Uncle Filimore said it best, I think. . ." Silas continued.

Jake looked around. It would be handy to have a wise uncle, but hell. Now he knew what he wanted. What he needed.

His eyes drifted to Ella. The first chance he had, he'd tell her that.

Ella whispered, "Looks like we have it under control." Then she stood and spoke in a louder voice. "Oh! I think the light is just perfect for those flowers over by the sidewalk. I'll be right back, honey. Meet back in the room soon?"

That was the signal for him to take his break, and he forced his voice to be light. "Sure."

She was right, of course; the speeches were likely to go on for a while, and he would have to be extra alert later, with the comings and goings that would begin when the meal was served. There were two big guys at the lobby doors and several more scattered around the grounds — the extra security detail Silas had hired for the day — so now was as good a time as ever.

"See you, honey," he called, releasing Ella's hand at the last possible second.

We'll talk once we get this reception out of the way and everything settles down. I promise I'll explain.

Jake jutted his jaw to one side, hoping Ella wouldn't change her mind. He rode the elevator up, entered the suite, and immediately grimaced. Housekeeping had been through and erased every hint of the previous night. The bed was made with tight, crisp sheets, stealing any hints of the intimacy he and Ella had shared the previous night. The coffee table was lined up with the couch again, the pillows back in place and fluffed. No champagne bucket. Not even a puddle to remind him of the best part. Everything was shiny and sterile, as if he had imagined it all.

He flopped down on a chair on the balcony, picking up the puzzle box for something to occupy his mind. If he tried to do nothing for ten straight minutes, he would go nuts.

Up. Left. Down. He pushed one row of squares sideways and another column up, rearranging the moving pieces in the eight-by-eight section of the lid. One of these days, he'd get that box open and find out what was inside. Even if it was empty, that would be okay. He would just scramble the pattern and try all over again. Or maybe he would find himself another puzzle box and–

Something clicked, and the lid pressed slightly against his thumb. It didn't open, but he must be close. He leaned over the box, rearranging another couple of blocks. Three moves later, he'd moved the ivory piece two spots down and one over from the mahogany square, like a knight on a chessboard. Then he slid another section left, moving the sandalwood block closer to the middle, and—

Click! The lid popped open under his hand.

He stared for a minute, amazed he had finally cracked the code. A little deflated too, because what would he have to keep busy with after that?

He pushed the lid open. It was thick and heavy, housing a hidden mechanism that allowed the wooden blocks to move around and trip the lock. That only left about an inch of height in the lower portion of the box, and that was divided into four squares. Three were empty, but the fourth was stuffed with a white cloth.

Looking up, he nearly said, *Ella, check this out.*

But there was no one there. No one to share this minor victory with.

The cloth turned out to be a little pouch, soft all over except for an oblong lump in the middle. The light padding had kept whatever it was from bumping around and making a sound. Did the lady who sold him the puzzle box know there was something in there? Jake loosened the noose looped around the bag, hoping it wasn't some kind of family heirloom that would require him to track the lady down to make sure she got it back.

"Come out already," he murmured, pulling a wad of cotton out of the pouch. Then he carefully unfolded that to reveal what was inside.

Not a pearl. Not a marble. More like an oblong pebble, but the colors. . .

Jake held his breath as a ray of sunlight caught on the face of the stone. Parts of it were pink, others white, still others green — a whole rainbow of colors swirling through the rock. He pursed his lips in a cutoff whistle. Whatever kind of stone that was — an opal, maybe? — it was a doozy. The color shone blue when he angled his hand one way but changed to orange when he tilted it. Orange like the outer ring of Ella's eyes. He tilted it left and right, wondering if—

His head snapped up in alarm. Not from anyone or anything in particular but from a tightening feeling in his gut. A bad, *brace yourself soldier* kind of feeling he had only felt a couple of times. The sense of impending doom, of a missile about to explode.

He stood quickly, pocketing the stone, and stood perfectly still, trying to get a handle on what was wrong. But there was nothing — no scream, no explosion, no revving engine or out-of-control truck. Still, his heart thumped and his blood rushed. Something was wrong. Something was definitely wrong.

He rushed downstairs, taking the stairs instead of the elevator, and those, four at a time. The second he burst into the lobby, a babble of concerned voices hit his ears.

"Get her a drink."

"Call an ambulance."

"Put her feet up."

He rushed toward the source of the commotion in the ballroom.

"I told you those babies were coming," one of the older ladies observed.

Boone looked like he was about to have a heart attack. Nina was pale but calmly assuring all the people clustered around her she was fine, just fine. And finally, it clicked. Nina was in labor. But that wouldn't set off this crazy danger reflex, would it? Jake whirled, surveying the scene.

Hunter spoke urgently into a phone. Silas was waving guests back, giving Nina space.

"Get the car," someone said.

"No, get an ambulance."

"Honestly, I'm fi—" Nina bit off the last word with a gasp and held her belly.

"Ambulance," Boone barked. "Stay calm, honey," he said to Nina, though he was the one who was white as a sheet.

"I'm so sorry," Nina said, clutching Cassandra's hand.

"Are you kidding?" Cassandra grinned. "Perfect excuse to move this event along. And I can't wait to meet your babies. I bet you can't either."

Nina beamed, gasped, and finally smiled again.

Jake hurried toward the lobby doors, because that ruckus wasn't the problem. Not that Nina going into labor wasn't a big deal, but that didn't account for the *man all stations* alarms in his mind. He rushed outside, looking around.

"Where's Ella?" he asked Kai.

Kai motioned vaguely as he barked into his phone. "When can you get the ambulance here?"

Jake dashed onto the lawn, looking everywhere, shouting for Ella in his mind. Where was she? What was going on?

A flash of red sped down the driveway and disappeared from sight, and Jake's first impression was that must have been Boone, speeding Nina to the hospital in the Ferrari. But he'd just seen Boone in the ballroom, so—

He spun around then sprinted over to Toby — now back in valet mode — who strode over, grinning broadly. "You must be so excited."

Not really, no. Nina was getting the help she needed. But where the hell was Ella?

"A honeymoon and a new property, right here on Maui," Toby said, nodding cheerily. "Man, some guys can only wish."

"The property isn't really mine," he murmured, wondering how Toby knew about the property Ella, Kai, and Hunter had inherited from their foster mother. He paced right past Toby, because that wasn't important right now. "Anyway, my wife is selling it."

My wife. Jake shocked himself with how earnestly he'd uttered the word.

Toby looked confused. "You mean, buying it. I thought that's what he said."

"Selling," Jake grunted, looking around. He, she — Toby was obviously confused. But, man. Couldn't the kid see he didn't have time to chat right now?

He started to walk away, but Toby's words stopped him dead in his tracks. "Your wife is feeling better, right?"

Jake spun on a dime. "What do you mean?"

Toby motioned vaguely. "Well, when she fainted—"

"When she *what*?"

Toby motioned over his shoulder. "Just a few minutes ago. She wilted, just like that. A good thing that guy was with her."

Jake's mind spun. Ella didn't faint. Ella didn't even yawn. She never showed weakness of any kind. Maybe the clueless kid had gotten Ella mixed up with Nina going into labor or something.

"She's fine. The ambulance is coming to take her to the delivery room."

Toby shook his head. "Not Ms. Miller. Your wife. She fainted, right over there." He pointed to a copse of trees at the edge of the lawn.

Jake's heart jackhammered away. "Where is she now?"

Toby motioned toward the parking lot. "Someone helped her over to the shade."

"Someone?" he demanded, a heartbeat away from sprinting to the parking lot. Did Toby mean Boone? Kai? Hunter, maybe? "The big guy?"

Toby nodded. "Yeah, that big guy. The one with the red SUV."

Jake stood still. Hunter usually drove the Land Rover. "Big guy, brown hair, brown beard?"

Toby stared at him. Jesus, it was like playing charades with a chipmunk.

"No, no beard. The other man. The realtor."

Nothing Toby was saying made sense. "What realtor?

"The really tall dude with a shaved head."

Jake was on the verge of saying the realtor looked nothing like that when it hit him who did, and his mind spun.

Red SUV, hightailing it out of the resort. Tall guy. Shaved head.

His stomach lurched. Gideon Goode?

Jake raced for the parking lot; Toby trailed behind. "What's wrong?"

Everything was wrong. Ella didn't faint, for starters. Gideon Goode had no business on the resort grounds, and he wasn't a realtor. And finally—

Jake stopped in the middle of the parking lot and pivoted in every direction. "What shade?"

Toby caught up, puffing, and pointed. "Over there."

Over there was a leaning palm tree with no one in sight. Jake raced over and toed the rut marks in the ground. The marks of a heavy vehicle with an interlocking, toothy tread. Something glinted underfoot, and he crouched, picking it out of the mud.

"What is it?" Toby asked.

Jake picked the tangle apart with shaking fingers. A plain silver necklace. Ella's necklace.

The next instant, he was sprinting for the pink Jeep with it and groping under the carpet for the key. A second later, he revved the engine to life and accelerated out of the parking lot. The tires squealed as disapproving guests shot him dirty looks, but he ignored them. The resort gates were open as an ambulance rolled in, and Jake swerved around it, fishing for the phone in this pocket. Moments later, he peeled onto the highway and accelerated while hitting buttons on the phone.

"Come on," he muttered, hoping Kai would pick up. "Come on. . ."

Chapter Fourteen

Ella sucked in a sharp breath and kicked out into the darkness. But her leg barely moved, and everything was foggy. Worse than foggy – everything was black, as if a blanket had been thrown over her. Her shoulders ached. The taste of bile filled her mouth, and her head spun. What was going on? Why was she lying down?

She tried to reach for her face, but her hands were stuck behind her. A low, grumbling chuckle sounded, neither near nor far. Somehow the distance was impossible to judge.

"How long does that stuff work?" a gruff voice she didn't recognize asked.

"Depends on the shifter. But seeing as she's just a little fox, it could last another few minutes," an even deeper voice said.

Hey, she wanted to protest. *I'm not little.*

But she couldn't speak, and she could barely move. With her hands bound behind her back, all she could manage was a weak wiggle. That made the nausea well up again, so she gave up except for rolling sideways. She might throw up, but at least she wouldn't choke on her own vomit.

"You sure she's a fox?" the other man asked.

The deep voice chuckled. "Trust me. I've got the best nose in the shifter world."

"Well, I think she's coming out of it."

Coming out of what? All Ella remembered was making a quick patrol of the grounds at the resort. Silas's speech about love and destiny had tugged every frayed string in her heart, making all her emotions bubble to the surface at the same time. So she had hurried outside to distance herself from all those happily mated couples while they celebrated something she could never have.

Jake. She wanted to whisper his name. To reach for his hand, to look into his eyes. To explain. That morning, she'd been ready to search for some way to make their relationship work. But then Kai had called to check in about the day, and gradually, the folly of her fantasy became clear. If she really loved Jake, she would let him go. The fact that she wanted to cry for his help right now was just another reason to call it quits. He made her weak. Unfocused. Unprofessional.

Fragments of memories raced through her mind, all mixed up and ragged around the edges. A foul smell. An evil grin. Footsteps. . .

Her body froze as a face emerged from the fog in her mind. Gideon Goode, the shifter who had come to see the property on Pu'u Pu'eo. The one she assumed had business connections with Silas. Had Silas misjudged his allies — or had she connected the wrong dots?

He'd stepped out of his SUV in the parking lot of the Kapa'akea Resort, dressed to the nines in a suit tailored to his giant frame. She'd gone over to check his invitation and, shit — fallen for a trap.

Miss Kitt. What a surprise to see you here, he'd said, smooth as can be.

Mr. Goode. Invitation, please.

She'd even held out her hand, grudgingly expecting him to be legit. But Goode had pulled a handkerchief out of his pocket, not an invitation, and covered his mouth as if to sneeze. Then he'd gestured over her shoulder and—

She made a face, recalling what little there was of the rest. She'd turned to see what he was indicating — total amateur move — just in time to hear footsteps and the hissing sound of spray. A burning stench had filled her nose, making the world spin and her knees buckle. She hadn't even gotten a look at the man who'd snuck up behind her, just a lungful of that obnoxious smell. And then she was falling. . . falling. . .

Gotcha, honey, Goode had chuckled, picking her up like a rag doll.

"Gotcha," he murmured now.

Something warm touched her leg, and she jerked away. Then the vehicle hit a bump, and she bounced on the seat.

Shit, a vehicle. Goode was taking her somewhere — never a good scenario, even if it did mean her friends weren't in danger at the moment. But, crap. She sure was.

The weight pressed over her leg again — a wide, callused hand — and she flinched as it stroked up and down. The car swerved and Goode chuckled, making her skin crawl as much as his touch did.

"Nice little fox we got here. An unexpected bonus to this entire trip, wouldn't you say, Burman?"

She jerked away, trying to force her eyes open. But the second she did, another wave of nausea made her squeeze them shut again.

"What will the boss say about that?" the second, more nasal voice — Burman, she supposed — asked.

Goode slammed the dashboard with a fist and roared, "Moira is not my boss, you got that?"

Ella jerked her head around. Moira?

"Sorry," Goode's accomplice murmured. "But Moira wanted us to take out the pregnant one, right?"

Ella's eyes went wide. *No, not Nina. Please, not Nina...*

Goode grumbled. "There's no way we'd get close to that bitch. What Moira wanted was to send a clear message to the shifters here, and we've done that. Meanwhile, I get to take care of my own wish list. A win-win. You get that?"

"I get it, I get it," the second man rushed to agree. "So Moira gets the fox—"

"I get the fox," Goode boomed. "She fits in perfectly with what I already have running. Moira gets what she asked for — and nothing more."

Ella's mind spun. So Silas's fears were founded — Moira had targeted the shifters of Koa Point once again. She hadn't dared launch a strike at the estate, but obviously, she'd had enough money to hire Goode, who also harbored some grudge...

"And how are you going to get this fox off the island?" Burman asked after a minute ticked by.

Ella flicked her ears, holding her breath.

Goode snorted. "Have I taught you nothing? It's just a slight change of plan. All I need is a private jet. She'll more than earn back the cost once I make her available to my customers. But first things first." Ella flinched as his hand landed on her leg again, this time above her knee. "We use our bait to pull in McBride and finish him. Then we can move on to our next target. And the next, and the next, until that entire unit gets what they deserve."

She froze. Jake? What did he want with Jake?

"Like Hoover?" Burman snorted. "We can take him out any time. No problem."

Goode gave her hip an affectionate pat and finally left her alone. "They deserve it for fucking up my delivery, and they're going to pay. The second we finish off that unit, we can get back to business. With a new asset, no less."

Ella had often been referred to as a tactical asset. But Goode's tone hinted at something completely different. Something that made her sick.

She forced her eyes open. At first, everything was blurry. Then two lumpy forms and a slice of light took shape — the front seats of the SUV. She had been thrown across the back seat. Peering down, she saw a thick cord of rope wrapped around her ankles. Her dress had ridden up, and she flinched, instinctively moving her hands to yank the hem down. But her hands were bound behind her back, and the motion only made pain flare through her shoulders.

Fuck. How could she have let this happen?

She thought it over, kicking herself for letting her guard down. Silas's speech had gone right to her heart, and all she could think of was Jake.

It's time to think about survival, she ordered herself.

But, damn. Even now, she couldn't stop thinking about him. The pull of her mate was that powerful, that all-consuming...

Get your head in the game, Kitt, she barked.

134

A phone chimed, and the man in the passenger seat clicked it on. "Hello? Yes, all set." He checked his watch. "ETA approximately thirty minutes."

Ella twisted her wrists, but it was no use. Whoever had tied those knots knew what he was doing, and movement only made the rope chafe deeper into her skin. Shifting into fox form wouldn't help her, not with her arms pinned behind her back. She would dislocate both shoulders if she tried. Shifter healing was fast, but not instantaneous. She'd be more helpless than she was now.

She gnashed her teeth. She didn't do *helpless*. She didn't do *victim*. She was a warrior, dammit.

So, think, she chided herself. *Think fast.*

She wiggled along the seat, trying to gain some sense of where the car was heading and how long she had been unconscious. A peek between the front seats gave her a glimpse of the clock on the dashboard. It was 3:18, so she hadn't blacked out for long. The roll of tires was fast enough to indicate they were on the highway. The sun flashed between trees, creating a strobe-like effect that made the nausea worse.

Weapons. Communications. Ammo? She made a quick mental check of what she had. Which was pretty much zilch. She had dropped her phone somewhere along the line, and the only weapon her honeymooner role allowed was the knife strapped to her thigh. She rolled slowly to the left until the hilt pressed into her thigh. At least she had that. The question was how to get to it.

Goode readjusted the rearview mirror to look at her, and — too late — she flicked her eyes away.

"Ah. Miss Kitt. So nice to see you again."

"Speak for yourself, asshole."

He grinned. "I hate to have pulled you away from that touching occasion. Nothing more beautiful than a couple of shifters finding eternal love." His voice dripped sarcasm.

The man in the passenger seat snorted, and Ella found herself wanting to punch them both. Love wasn't something to mock. It was a treasure, as Georgia Mae had always said.

"What do you want?"

Goode chuckled. "I want a lot of things. But it's a long story. Maybe I'll tell you after."

She narrowed her eyes, wishing she could read his thoughts. After what?

Goode readjusted the rearview mirror, checking the road behind him, and Burman swiveled around to do the same. "No sign of him yet."

Ella's stomach sank. No sign of whom? Jake? But why?

"Maybe you should slow down a little," Burman murmured.

They wanted to be followed? Who the hell did that?

Ella closed her eyes and reached out to her shifter friends. *Boone. Kai.*

No answer.

Silas! Hunter?

One after another, she tried reaching each one.

Cruz... Tessa... Dawn? Anyone!

Usually, it took a moment or two to establish the kind of mental connection needed to push her thoughts into her friends' minds. But she was still dizzy, and something else was going on. Something chaotic that had Kai, Hunter, and the others throwing orders at each other. Shit. Had there been some kind of attack?

"We could not have asked for a better diversion." Burman laughed.

Goode nodded. "Yeah — and a better insurance policy." He glanced back at Ella. "I have an extra man standing by. Any trouble from you and those babies are dead."

She froze. Nina's babies? "What kind of monster are you?"

Goode just laughed and tossed one hand up. "You know how it is. Life is cheap. It comes, it goes."

Her jaw went slack. Those were babies, for goodness' sake. "If you touch them..."

"Don't make that necessary, and I won't. You understand?"

She was tempted to call his bluff, because no one was getting past Boone, Hunter, and the others to threaten those babies. But, hell. She wasn't about to gamble with innocent lives.

Holding perfectly still, she closed her eyes and tried reaching out to her friends again. The nausea was subsiding, but the chaos on their end went on, making it impossible to break through with a plea for help. Which she loathed to do anyway. She didn't call for the cavalry. She *was* the cavalry.

Except right now. She was trussed up like a goddamn goose instead of getting ready to blaze in for a rescue with her guns blazing.

Jake, her fox whispered.

She closed her eyes and pictured his face, doing her best to tap into his mind. But humans weren't trained in the fine art of opening their minds to the thoughts of others, and all she sensed was a vague cloud of anxiety and concern.

God, what could she do? She needed help, but Jake couldn't take on two shifters. As a human, he stood no chance.

Goode twisted to look back then flicked his eyes down to Ella. His eyes swept over her body, undressing her, and he grinned. *Grinned,* like she was going to smile back or something. When he reached out, she wiggled backward, but there was nowhere to go. All she could do was clamp her legs firmly together while Goode dragged a finger from her hip to her knee. Then he held his finger under his nose, sniffed deeply, and scowled.

"McBride," he grunted, displeased.

Ella gritted her teeth. Of course, a shifter could pick up on the little bit of Jake's scent lingering on her body. Even a shower couldn't erase that after all they'd done.

"I told you." Burman laughed.

"Lucky man," Goode conceded. "He must have enjoyed a hell of a night. But I suppose it's tradition to grant a condemned man his last wish."

Ella thrashed at the back of Goode's seat. "You leave him alone!"

"You think I came all the way to Maui just to say hi and goodbye?" Goode sneered. "I came to cut his throat, and I will do it. A man who fucks with another man's business deal – a deal worth millions – doesn't get to walk away."

Ella's heart hammered away. Jake was a good soldier. A good man. But Goode — Jesus, the man was insane.

Goode checked his watch and motioned to Burman. "Get me that jet. I want it ready by six. Seven at the latest."

"Might be hard to arrange at this short notice," Burman warned.

"Just do it," Goode roared, turning red. The man had a fuse about a quarter of an inch long. "And when you're done, get Norris on the line. I want to tell him the good news." Goode grinned, swinging through another sharp mood shift and looking back at her.

Ella's skin crawled. The man was out of his mind.

"Oh, I won't kill you, sweetheart," he said, misreading her expression. "You're much more valuable to me alive. But that human isn't worth anything. In fact, he owes me five million dollars. And since I doubt that country boy has that much in his account, he'll pay with his life, as they all have."

"Except Hoover," the other guy pointed out. "And the other four—"

"To hell with Hoover!" Goode exploded, making Burman jump. A second later, Goode straightened his collar and went on in a measured voice. "I might not even kill Hoover. I couldn't pay someone to be as useful as he's turned out to be. It's almost been fun to watch him make everyone paranoid."

Ella gulped. It sure wasn't fun watching Goode. What a madman.

The SUV slowed for the next light and came to a stop beside a truck. Ella looked up, desperately signaling the driver with her eyes. But the windows on Goode's vehicle were tinted, so no one could see her — and just as well. What good would it do to drag a human into this?

Her stomach turned. Jake was a human, too.

The vehicle accelerated and she listened in as Burman murmured into his phone. "A four-seater would be fine. By seven o'clock. Yes, Houston." He covered the mouthpiece with his hand and looked at Goode. "Changing in LA?"

Goode shook his head, looking positively lethal. "Do better, Burman."

Burman hurried back to whomever he had on the line. "The boss wants a direct flight. Do it." He listened for a while, then nodded. "Right. And tell our supplier we're bringing in a new asset to join the other girls."

Ella's jaw fell open. Where these madmen running some kind of sex ring?

Goode glanced at her, all smiles again. "I can already see what they'll pay for you."

Ella kicked his seat and bared her teeth. If they were thinking of selling her as a sex slave, they had another thing coming. Like having their balls ripped off.

But Goode just laughed. "A feisty female shifter. A fox, no less."

Her eyes shot daggers at him, but Goode just went on.

"Perfect look. Keep that up. My customers love a woman who can put up a good fight. It makes them feel more accomplished when they finally get what they want." His eyes glowed with arousal as if he could picture the scene. Worse — as if he could picture himself in that scene.

Ella cringed. She was a capable fighter, for sure. But Goode had taken her by surprise, and if he kept her tied up, there was little she could do. Her mind spun for some means of escape. He would have to let her out of the SUV at some point, and if she was quick. . .

Escape isn't enough, her fox cut in. *I want revenge.*

No kidding. The second Ella got loose – somehow – she would turn on Goode with her claws unsheathed. Goode might have a size advantage in human and shifter form, but she knew tricks to work around that.

She took a deep breath. Realistically, whatever chance she got would be brief, and she would have to act fast. She played out a dozen different scenarios in her mind, most starting with reaching her knife. She would yank it from its sheath, plunge it deep into Goode's heart and twist, making sure he bled out fast enough to render his shifter healing powers ineffectual. Then she would have to shift to fox form to attack the second man. A plan with too many *ifs*, but what else could she do?

She swung her feet to the floor and tensed her stomach muscles, heaving through the equivalent of an abdominal crunch to sit up in the back seat.

Goode nodded ahead. "Nice view, eh?"

Her eyes darted around, trying to establish her bearings. Goode drove straight past the airport and continued on Highway 350 – the road to Hana. Almost immediately, the road narrowed and curved with every contour of the dramatic coastline. The road home.

Ella frowned. Home. It had been bad enough to see Goode step foot on her property before. To have him bring her there like a trussed-up trophy was hard to bear.

"Home sweet home, little fox," Goode said, confirming her fears. "That piece of shit property is the perfect place for what I have in mind."

Her mouth hung open. Why was he taking her to Pu'u Pu'eo? The off-the-beaten-track homestead might be a good place to keep a hostage hidden for a week or two, but Goode had been talking about a flight. So what was he up to?

Jake, her fox cried. *He wants to kill Jake there.*

Her blood ran cold. All the factors that made the homestead the ideal shifter home — the remote location, thick forest, and absence of neighbors — also made it the ideal place for a shifter fight. No human would stumble across them there.

Kai! Hunter! she called through her mind. She boiled down the situation to its basics and tried to communicate it to them through images of the property they'd all grown up on. Sooner or later, Kai and Hunter would pick up on that, and—

Later might be too late, her fox barked.

"Almost there. . . " Goode murmured, taking a sharp turn.

Sitting up made her feel less like a sack of potatoes, but it hurt like hell, what with her arms tied behind her back. Every time Goode swung the SUV around a left curve, she bumped into the right-side door and wrenched her shoulders. When Goode swung the vehicle right, she threatened to topple over.

She twisted to look around. The trunk was empty except for two travel duffels. No weapons of torture, no automatic guns. Goode looked ready for a quick departure, and soon.

Right after, he'd said.

As in, after Jake's death. She was sure of it now.

Not letting that happen, her inner fox vowed.

The car swung through another few turns, each as familiar to her as the back of her hand. There was Peahi, where a couple of dozen surfers bobbed offshore, waiting for a perfect wave. On the right, vegetation tangled the hills, forming a thick wall of tropical forest she had explored as a kid. They passed a twin-forked waterfall where a tour bus stopped for passengers to snap pictures. When the SUV slowed and bumped off the paved road, her inner alarms clanged harder. The gears groaned and the chassis squeaked as Goode put the SUV in four-wheel drive and headed uphill. Jesus, he really was bringing her home.

Our home turf, her fox growled. *Our advantage.*

Sure — if she could move around. She twisted her wrists harder, ignoring the burning pain.

"You know what would be poetic justice?" Burman chuckled to Goode. "If you actually bought this place."

Goode laughed. "No, piece of shit shacks are not my thing. It's not even worth half the asking price."

Ella strained at her bonds, vowing to throttle them both. It was ridiculous to allow a madman's words to sting her so deeply, but they did. That little cottage meant more to her than she could ever explain — something Jake had understood and respected right away. It didn't matter that she had always pined for the desert Southwest. She knew to appreciate Maui for all it had given her. A loving home. A stable life. A family that accepted her as she was.

But Goode didn't respect anything, and having him step foot on the property felt as wrong to Ella as a slap in Georgia Mae's honest, hardworking face.

"Patel," Goode called in greeting to a tall man with long, fair hair waiting beside the gate.

When Goode stopped outside the car, Burman slid out of the SUV, gave the chain a quick yank, and shoved the gate open. He held up the broken chain with a grin that said, *See my power? See what I can do?*

Ella rolled her eyes. She had shifter powers too. And that chain was rusty. He'd have to do a lot more to impress her.

A second later, the door to the SUV was flung open. Goode grabbed her ankle, hauled her out like a reluctant fish, and threw her over his shoulder with a firm pat on her ass. "Don't test me, honey. Believe me, you don't want to see me get mad."

A deep, burning hate warmed her blood, and it took everything she had to stay still. Inside, she vowed revenge. The second she had her chance, Goode would be dead.

There was a certain amount of bravado in the thought, she knew, considering Goode's size. But if she didn't believe in herself, she was surrendering herself to a horrible fate, and she'd never give in. Never.

The familiar scents of home washed over her, but it all felt so wrong, and not just due to her upside-down view. Patel, the third man, stole off to one side, stomping through the remnants of Georgia Mae's herb garden. Burman kicked over the wooden tiki Hunter had carved when he was fourteen and then walked ahead. "You want her on the porch where he can see her?"

"Nah. I'll put her inside. On the bed, where she belongs."

If Ella's hands had been free, she would have gouged his eyes out. But all she could do was bump along, steeling herself to make a move the moment Goode put her down.

But Goode, dammit, anticipated as much. He stomped up the stairs, strode through the small house, and kicked open a door. Then he threw her on Georgia Mae's creaky bed and pinned her down. He leaned over her, coming to within an inch of her face, grinning madly.

"You want to escape, sweetheart? You want to play?"

She could sense his inner shifter growling, itching for a hunt. The man was a monster. Terrifying.

"Some game," she muttered, turning her face to the side.

Goode grabbed her chin, forcing her to face him. His foul breath washed over her, and his hands tightened over her shoulders. "Oh, a chase will be fun. I promise you."

"You're sick."

Goode grinned and put a hand on her stomach. "Maybe I'll have a different kind of fun with you first. My customers like fresh meat, but I reckon you'll have some fight left over—"

He snapped his head up at the sound of tires scattering gravel. Distant and so faint, only sensitive shifter ears could catch the sound, but definitely headed toward the homestead.

"He's coming," Burman called, more amused than alarmed.

Goode broke into a wide grin and pulled away. "Perfect."

Before Ella could execute the knee-in-the-balls move she had planned, Goode stunned her with a heavy slap and re-arranged her bonds to secure her to the bed frame. Seconds later, he stomped toward the door.

Ella screamed inside. *No, Jake. No! Get the others. Get help! Don't risk yourself.*

But it was too late. Jake barely made a sound, but the wind had carried his scent, and her fox ears flicked at the faint sound of careful footsteps padding through the surrounding forest.

Goode chuckled in anticipation. "McBride."

Chapter Fifteen

Jake ran in a crouch, stopping behind one tree before dashing to the next. Then he stopped cold at the sound of his name.

"We know you're out there," Goode announced in that arrogant tone.

Jake frowned. He hadn't been making a sound. How the hell had Goode picked up on his approach?

He straightened slowly. So much for the element of surprise — the only advantage he had. Clicking his fingers over his phone, he dialed Kai one more time. He'd been trying to reach Boone and Kai throughout the drive — the only two guys whose numbers he had. Every good soldier knew better than to rush into enemy territory without backup or a solid plan. But, shit. Neither Boone nor Kai was picking up. Too busy with the baby emergency, it seemed.

Well, this was an emergency too. Ella had been taken, and every second counted. It was a miracle he'd found his way to the remote property, especially since he hadn't been paying much attention the one time Ella drove him there. But at every confusing intersection or hidden turn, he'd known where to go as sure as if a navigation unit had been pointing the way. Somehow, he could feel Ella out there, and that drew him on.

"Damn it," he muttered, pocketing the phone. Then he strode out into the open and stepped onto the lower edge of the sloping property. No flak vest, no helmet, no weapon. Just a spinning mind and a hammering heart.

"About time you came." Goode stood high and mighty on the front porch, establishing his position immediately. I *am boss here, and you have no chance.*

Jake didn't blink. Goode might be the boss of the man standing at the foot of the stairs, but he sure as hell wasn't Jake's boss. Both Goode and the other guy appeared unarmed and supremely confident of...what? Tearing him to pieces with their bare hands?

Something in the way Goode's eyes shone suggested that wasn't far off.

"Where is she?" Jake demanded.

"Got her right where I want her." Goode sneered.

"The hell you do," Ella barked from somewhere inside the house.

Jake took half a step forward before he caught himself. Thank God Ella was alive. Conscious, too, and obviously pissed off. He pictured the layout of the house, trying to pinpoint her.

Goode laughed. "Feisty little thing. Just how I like them." Then he called to Ella and adjusted the crotch of his pants. "Don't worry, sweetheart. You won't have to wait long. I'll be right in."

Jake gritted his teeth. Goode was goading him. He had to cut emotion out of the equation if he was going to find a way out of this.

"You and that asshole yes-man of yours, Burman?" she snapped back. "Or do you mean Patel, wherever he is?"

Three men, then. Jake looked around. Goode and a black-haired guy — Burman, he assumed — stood at the bottom of the stairs, but the third was hiding somewhere. *Go, Ella,* for keeping her head together and conveying that information to him. Of course, with Ella, he expected no less. Her words also indicated she wasn't being guarded, so she might have some way of working herself free from however they had her tied or cuffed.

Jake snapped his attention back to his adversaries as the third man, Patel, emerged from where he'd been concealed. A tall guy with long, fair hair. For a moment, all Jake could see was a silhouette, and he shook off the feeling of it being familiar somehow. The only thing that mattered right now was buying Ella time to get free. Of course, it would only take those two one squeeze of a trigger, and he'd be dead. But the weird thing was, neither of them had pulled a weapon yet.

"You wanted this property so bad, you kidnapped the owner?" he asked, glancing around surreptitiously for something he could use as a weapon.

Goode loomed over the scene from the front porch, arms crossed, a wicked grin on his face. "There's so much you don't understand."

Jake had no desire to talk to the guy, but he had to keep Goode talking — and ideally, coax him down from the porch to pull his attention away from Ella. "Then why don't you explain?"

Goode didn't signal, but Burman nodded and started circling around Jake. Sizing him up, flashing an obnoxious, *I know something you don't know* grin.

Jake turned slowly with him, keeping one eye on Goode and Patel, who didn't budge.

"Collateral damage. You know what that means?" Goode called out as Burman reached a point behind Jake, forcing him to jerk around in order to keep everyone in his sights. Every muscle in his body tensed. It would have been the perfect moment for them to jump him from opposite sides, but Goode seemed content to draw the tension out.

Jake didn't bother to answer. Of course he knew what collateral damage was.

"That's what you might call Miss Kitt."

Jake clenched his fists. The hell, she was.

"You touch her, and I'll—"

"Oh, but I have." Goode leered. "I plan to do a lot more touching, in fact. The funny thing is, I didn't come to Maui for her."

Jake forced himself to keep his inner soldier engaged and not the gorilla that urged him to rush Goode then and there. Something glinted behind Patel — the machete Jake had left stuck in a stump before. He calculated how many steps it would take him to get there, but he didn't make a move. Yet.

A bird swooped overhead, casting a shadow over him, then fluttered into the woods.

"So you came for...?" Jake murmured, only half paying attention while he tried to cobble together some kind of plan.

Goode laughed. "I came for you."

Jake stopped abruptly. What the fuck?

He would have said that, too, if it hadn't been for that bird fluttering back. Lower this time, sweeping right over Burman's head. The black-haired man ducked and cursed as the bird hurtled toward the porch, right at Goode. A big owl with mottled gray wings that matched the shadows of the forest.

"Bitch," Goode uttered, slapping the air with his hand.

The owl veered away and landed on the low branch of a giant monkeypod tree on one side of the property.

Jake eyed Goode. Bitch? Of all the things to call a bird...

He put a hand over his right pants pocket because, damn. His thigh was itchy under there. Really itchy, like the time Manny had slipped a hot chili pepper into his pocket in one of many practical jokes.

Patel stepped away from Goode's side, moving through the dappled light, and Jake froze. He knew that guy. Tall man, long hair. The driver of the car that had tried to run him down?

His mind spun. So that hadn't been a prank. But what the hell did they want?

"You came for me?" Jake held his arms up in surrender. "You got me. Let Ella go. She has nothing to do with this."

Goode smirked. "Ah, but she does. Moira wanted to send Silas a message that she could strike anywhere, anytime, and that's done. Even better, the little fox means something to you. She means a lot to you, I suspect. Which is why I am going to take her away, just to even the score."

Jake's mind spun. Moira. Fox? What did Goode mean?

"Even the score," Jake echoed in a perfectly flat voice. He didn't even know the guy.

A second owl flew into view — so big, the air whistled around its wings. The bird curved around Jake, swept right over Burman, making him duck, and made a graceful landing on a tree opposite the other owl. There, it shook out its wings and stared at Burman with huge, intelligent eyes.

Just a couple of friends of mine, Ella had joked before.

It was uncanny, the way the birds gave Jake the sense of reinforcements creeping into position. But, hell. Friends of Ella were friends of his. If Goode and Patel were at twelve o'clock from his point of view, the owls were at three and nine o'clock. Burman was the second hand on that clock, sweeping around and around, keeping Jake on his toes. But the owls put Goode and his men on their toes, too, making them swivel their heads the way Jake had been doing. He wasn't confident that the owls would actually help, but he welcomed the distraction they provided.

Goode shot each bird a dark look and went on. "Of course, I have to even the score. Unless you have five million dollars. I'd be happy to take that instead."

The guy was nuts. Certifiably nuts. But the longer he talked, the more time Ella had to get free.

Come on, Ella, Jake urged in his mind.

The crazy thing was, he swore he sensed some kind of reply. Just a tickle at the edge of his mind, really, but somehow, it felt like Ella. Grunting something like, *Give me another minute, and I'll make these assholes sorry they were ever born.*

His right hand slipped to his leg, tempted to itch that hot spot on his thigh.

"Why would I give you five million?" he asked, turning on his heel to keep an eye on Burman.

"Because that's what you cost me that day in Kamdesh."

Jake froze. A stupid move, because if Burman or Patel had been paying closer attention, they could have capitalized on his surprise to jump in. Luckily, one owl screeched to the other just then, distracting them.

Kamdesh. The ambush. The day his unit had swapped positions with another vehicle that had gotten blown to bits.

I'm telling you, man. Someone is taking us out, one by one.

Jake stared at Goode. "The day my unit survived and another unit took the hit?" Did the lunatic want a million for each of the lives lost?

Goode scoffed. "Like it matters to me who lives and who dies. The money was supposed to get through. I had it all set up — the first vehicle with the money was supposed to get through while the others got hammered, but you ruined all that."

What money? Jake wanted to yell, but he was still reeling from the *like it matters to me who lives and who dies* part.

Goode checked his watch and snapped his fingers at his men. "Take care of him already. We've wasted enough time."

Patel grinned. "You mean the fun way, right?"

Jake grimaced, wondering what this guy's version of fun was. Would they back over him a few times with the heaviest truck they could find?

"The fast way," Goode snapped, then scowled at Jake. "Unless you want a deal?"

Jake made a face. Eyes didn't lie, and Goode's had death written in them. He could promise all he wanted; there would be no deal. At least, not one that ended with Goode upholding his end of things.

Still, to keep the clock ticking, he bluffed. "Sure. A deal. You let Ella go."

Goode laughed. "I love the noble warrior thing, don't you, boys?" The other two laughed. "That's why guys like you came back broke while we came home rich."

Jake tried to process that. Kamdesh. Five million. What kind of dirty deal had Goode been peddling? Drugs... prostitutes... weapons?

"Bastard," Jake spat.

In the blink of an eye, Goode went from cool and collected to crimson with rage. Apparently, *bastard* hit a nerve. "Get him. Kill him. Rip him to bits," he roared.

Jake took a step back. Whoa. The guy was nuts. Certifiably nuts. Then he jerked his head at a growling sound from the right, where Burman stood. An animal growl — and weirder still, the man's eyes glowed red. The hair on the back of Jake's neck rose when Burman bared his teeth and raised his arms.

150

Patel's chuckle made Jake turn back in that direction, where the man calmly removed his shirt and belt. The owl in the tree behind Patel fluttered its wings and shifted uneasily from foot to foot. When Burman groaned, Jake spun again, and—

"What the. . ." He trailed off. Burman was convulsing with a seizure of some kind.

"Those friends of yours," Goode yelled, taunting Jake. "The men of OD-X unit. Ever notice something funny about them?"

Jake stared as Burman dropped to all fours and curved his back. His shirt split down the middle, and the shadows that played over his bare skin took on a striped pattern.

"Something not quite human?" Goode went on, delighting in the bizarre scene. "Superhuman, you might say."

Jake tried to tune out Goode's chatter and wheeled around to check on Patel, who was down to briefs and calmly folding his pants over a nearby branch. The owl chirped viciously, and Goode's words stuck in Jake's mind.

Not quite human. . . Superhuman. . .

Yeah, he'd heard a few wild rumors about Silas's group. Rumors no sane man would believe.

He backed up two steps. The air crackled with energy, and his thigh itched. A low growl sounded from behind him, and when he turned—

Jake choked on his own exclamation. Burman was hairy as hell, and he had a tail. Stripes too. Huge white fangs.

Jake backed up slowly. Burman was a goddamn tiger, and he was snarling for blood.

"What the. . ." Jake jerked around.

Where Patel had been standing, a big, angry lion moved its tail in slow, greedy swipes.

Jake took another step back, grabbing the only weapon he could find — a sturdy branch from the stack he and Ella had made when they'd cleaned up the yard. The machete would have been a hell of a lot better, but that was all the way over by the porch. He jerked his head between the two felines, who lashed their tails and showed their teeth. Jesus, what was going on?

Goode cackled in glee. "Great weapon you got there, soldier."

Jake steeled his nerves and gripped the branch tighter. Ella. It was all for Ella. Maybe she could get away. Maybe Boone or Kai had finally received his messages and were on the way.

"Run while you can, soldier," Goode goaded. "Run while you can."

Jake gritted his teeth, keeping his back to the nearest tree. "Maybe you should run."

The lion and tiger stalked closer in smooth, swinging strides that made their shoulder blades rise with each step. Left, right. Left, right...

"Sure." Goode smirked. "As if those shifter friends of yours will come to the rescue. Humans are expendable. *You're* expendable. They won't bother to come help you. Oh, they might come for my feisty little fox..."

Goode motioned to the house. Did he mean Ella?

"...but by the time they do, she'll be long gone, working her new job. I might even visit her from time to time just for the satisfaction of knowing she was once yours."

"The hell you will," Jake spat, forcing his mind to quit trying to grasp it all and simply form some kind of plan to save Ella.

Goode snapped his fingers. "I said, get him!"

The lion coiled to jump. The tiger was a heartbeat faster, already airborne and hurtling toward Jake. Jake's eyes went wide at the huge white claws and flashing stripes, but his hands were steady on the thick branch he wielded, and when he connected with the tiger—

Smack! He batted the beast sideways.

The tiger yowled and rolled, reeling from the blow.

Jake didn't have time to stare at the branch and wonder if it was laced with kryptonite or something, because the lion was next. He jerked the branch to the right, backhanding the lion. Then he stared at the branch because, holy shit. His blows hadn't just made the beasts stumble — they sent the felines flying as if they were a quarter of their formidable bulks.

The heat in Jake's pocket intensified, and he couldn't help slipping his hand in to itch. His fingers pushed aside the pouch he'd stuck in his pocket earlier, and—

Whoa. The pouch was as warm as a hot potato. That was the source of the itch. Or rather, the opal was.

"What the hell..."

The felines growled and circled him, preparing for another attack. Goode heckled and swore. Jake planted his feet wide, trying to anticipate their next moves. Their next attack was more coordinated, with the lion closing in on one side and the tiger from the other, both growling under their breath.

"Try me," Jake muttered, telling himself it wasn't terrifying to be eye-to-eye with a couple of wild beasts of their size. That it wasn't weird to have an opal heat up in his pocket either. That he could handle this. He *had* to handle it.

The tiger roared and jumped, its jaws spread wide, fangs flashing. The air whooshed, and Jake heard himself yell. Something gray blurred behind the tiger, but he forced himself to focus on those killer jaws. He swung, putting all his strength into a blow that sent the beast sprawling to one side. Keeping the momentum going, Jake swung the branch in a huge arc. The lion was almost on him, about to pounce from behind, and he was sure he was too late. But that flash of gray fluttered between them, and the lion roared. The branch connected with the beast's muzzle a second later, and Jake and the beast stumbled apart. The lion jumped backward, roaring in anger at the sky.

An owl. That was an owl, and it had just saved Jake. The bird swooped higher to escape the lion while the second owl harried the beast.

"Goddammit!" Goode stamped on the porch steps, making them shudder. "Just kill him!"

Jake looked around. Apparently, the owls were on his side. Weird, but okay. He'd take what he could get. The heat in his pocket throbbed as if he'd just called for volunteers and another hand had shot up. What was up with that gemstone?

He didn't have time to puzzle that out, because the tiger was moving in again, more furious than ever. Faster too. Jake barely got the branch up to club the beast away when its claws ripped into his shoulder. Lightning bolts of pain shot through his nerves, and he fell backward.

Roll! part of his mind ordered. *Roll!*

He threw his weight to the left, grappling with the beast. He swatted desperately, trying to avoid the snapping jaws and clawing legs.

"Get him!" Goode yelled.

Push it! Shove it away! Jake barked at himself.

He heaved with all the force he could muster, and the tiger went flying — literally flying — and crashed into a tree, where it slumped. Jake rolled to his feet then immediately staggered, grabbing his shoulder. Warm, sticky blood trickled between his fingers. His leg hurt too, and a glance down showed a ragged red line below the knee of his pants.

Branch. Find the branch, he ordered himself, telling himself those were scratches and not gashes.

"Whoa," he muttered as he stooped for his makeshift club. One of the owls fluttered over him, screeching at an oncoming lion.

Oncoming lion, his hazy mind registered just in time to poke at it with the stick. It wasn't much of a hit, but it held the beast off long enough for the owl to swoop in, clawing at the lion's eyes. The lion scrambled away in retreat.

"Burman!" Goode yelled to his second accomplice.

Jake spun, ready to take on the tiger. But it was still slumped against the tree, barely stirring.

"Damn it!" Goode yelled. "Do I have to do everything myself?"

Jake squinted through the throb of pain he couldn't quite shake off. The curtains in the window behind Goode shifted, and Jake's heart leaped to his throat.

"Ella," he whispered, hoping she had found a way to get free and would escape out the back.

Then his attention jumped to Goode, who stripped his shirt off much like Patel had done before he'd turned into a wild beast.

Jake swung the branch from side to side, steeling himself for the worst. The heat in his pocket intensified, and strength seeped into his legs. He wouldn't kid himself about the extent of his injuries, but he didn't mind that extra boost, wherever it came from.

It comes from me, a little voice murmured in his mind as the gemstone sent out another bolstering shot of heat.

Jake blinked a few times. Shit, now he wasn't just seeing wild animals. He was hearing voices too.

Goode threw his shirt aside and snarled through frighteningly long teeth. The lion slunk backward with its tail low; the tiger struggled to its feet and swayed. Goode hunched, groaned, and began to transform. His legs bent back at the knees, and his spine stood out as the skin around it broke out in thick fur. When he ducked and shook his head, more hair emerged, forming an increasingly thick mane.

Jake's mouth hung open. Fuck. Another lion? Or was that a tiger? The tawny fur took on an orange hue near its rump, and the entire body was lined with dark stripes.

A lion. A tiger. A mix?

"You bastard," Jake whispered, testing it.

Goode roared furiously, confirming Jake's hunch. First, that Goode was in there and aware of human speech. And second, that Goode had to be some kind of bizarre mix between two species. One with a huge chip on his shoulder and no regard for human life.

One of the owls fluttered its tail feathers as if to say, *Oh, shit.*

Oh, shit was right. Goode was huge. Bigger than the biggest lion or tiger. He put one paw in front of the other, stalking toward Jake. His eyes glowed a murderous red, and he growled the entire time.

Die, that growl said. *You will die.*

Jake gripped his branch harder and showed his own teeth. But, damn. How much would a branch help? The machete would be better, but it looked farther away than ever. Even with it, he wasn't sure how much damage he could inflict on a beast of that size.

The owls launched themselves, one from either direction, harassing the beast. But Goode just swiped them away and strode onward, intent on Jake. The lion and limping tiger fell into step along his flanks, and they all converged on Jake.

What are you going to do now, asshole? Goode's growl asked.

A softer, higher snarl sounded from behind them, and Jake looked at the stairs.

Ella. He mouthed her name as he took in the coppery-blond fox growling from the top step. It was huge for a fox, but it still appeared petite. Feminine. The polar opposite of the felines converging on him now. The fox's orange-brown eyes flashed, and although Jake had no idea what was going on, he knew that was her.

"Ella," he whispered, holding back the *Run for your life* part because Ella didn't like to be told what to do.

The fox wagged its tail. Once. Twice. And suddenly, everything made sense.

I can't have you, Jake. I'm dangerous to you. Was this what Ella had meant?

The fox swung its tail and held its nose high, testing the air.

That's Burnam, and that's Patel, he was tempted to call out, but he didn't want to draw their attention to her. *And that ugly son of bitch in the middle is Goode.*

The fox bared its teeth and coiled, ready to attack from behind.

On three, its intelligent eyes said.

Jake's eyebrows shot up. A fox running a countdown?

Somehow, she made her plan clear with tiny movements. What she planned to do and which way she needed him to move, all subtly communicated in the way they had once in covert operations. And for about the hundredth time in Jake's life, he wished he could tell Ella how amazing she was.

Two, the fox's nod signaled.

Die, the snarling felines growled, unaware of her behind them.

Jake showed his teeth. "Try me, assholes."

Three, the fox snapped as all hell broke loose.

Chapter Sixteen

Ella launched herself at Goode with everything she had, powered by the anger and fear boiling over in her soul. That was her man out there, fighting on her behalf. Dying, if she didn't do anything about it. Jake's shoulder was stained red, his leg savaged, his eyes clouded with pain. Most humans looked like deer in headlights the first time they spotted shifters — not to mention shifters with a thirst for blood. Yet Jake managed to stand as solid as a rock, hefting that branch of his. A warrior to the last.

"Jake," she cried. But it came out a canine yelp, and he didn't understand.

Her wrists hurt like hell even now that she was in fox form, but that was nothing like the hurt to her pride. It had been a bitch to saw against the rusty edge of the bed's metal frame, but she'd done it. Now, she folded her ears back, coiled her muscles, and sprang at Goode's back. That had to be him — the sheer size gave him away. And no wonder she hadn't been able to identify his shifter species until now. He was a rare lion-tiger mix — a liger. An unnatural mix often called an abomination because those species never mixed in the wild. The beast combined the strength and ferocity of both species in a massive body that dwarfed any pure-blooded cat.

And damn it, he'd been toying with Jake. Well, she'd show him. No one messed with her man.

Yes, the liger was five times her size. No, she had no reason to believe she could overcome Goode or survive the afternoon. But at that moment, nothing mattered but helping her mate.

She snarled, digging her claws into Goode's back and chomping down on one ear. *Take that, asshole.*

The liger roared. He might have the size advantage, but she had the element of surprise. Was it sneaky coming up from behind? Hell yes. Payback for how Goode had tricked her back at the resort.

Now he'll pay the price, her fox snarled, shredding his ear.

But, crap. Even that fragile part of the liger was tough as leather. How was she ever going to vanquish that beast?

She bit harder and yanked, tearing through his flesh. The clearing erupted with the sounds of battle — snarls, roars, and her throaty growl — as Goode started to roll, intent on crushing her. Ella sprang away and rushed to Jake's side with a quickness and agility the liger could never match. For a second, she thought Jake would smack her with that branch, but when their eyes met, his mouth cracked open, and he froze.

Jake, she cried. *It's me. Your mate.*

She searched his eyes. Did he understand? Did he know why she'd had to push him away for so long?

"Ella," he whispered in awe.

All that transpired in the blink of an eye before they took up positions side by side, no longer lovers but comrades-in-arms. Like the last two goddamn soldiers guarding the Alamo, knowing they were going to pay with their lives.

She wagged her tail stiffly. Death didn't scare her. At least, not as much as the idea of living a long life without Jake. She snarled at the oncoming felines, and Jake yelled, "Back off!"

The massive feline shifters didn't back off, but they did pause. Even Goode hesitated at the force in Jake's voice. Hell, even Ella looked up. She had seen Jake shed his quieter, more reserved side in tight situations before, but never like this.

"I said back off, and get off this land!" he thundered.

Was that love powering him or something else?

Love, a faint voice said — a voice as old as the mountains. *My power is only a funnel for what lies within a soul.*

She stared. That voice wasn't Jake's, nor did it stem from one of the owls peering nervously down at the fight — distant relatives of Georgia Mae's who had always guarded this special place. It wasn't her inner fox either, and it sure wasn't Goode or his men.

When Jake pressed his right hand over his pocket, the air vibrated the way it might from a powerful bassline at a concert, except there was no sound.

Spirit Stone, her fox whispered in awe. *It has to be.*

But how? Jake didn't know the Spirit Stones existed, and Silas never would have loaned him one of the five kept safe at Koa Point.

Not a Spirit Stone, the voice whispered. *I am their maker.*

Ella's eyes went wide. Holy shit. The Keystone? Where had Jake found it? How? Why?

The voice didn't reveal anything, but in her heart, she knew. Destiny. It had to be destiny.

She wagged her tail hard enough to swat Jake's leg and lifted her chin. *Okay, destiny. You got us this far. Now get us the rest of the way.*

The ancient voice rumbled, *Destiny only puts events into motion. The rest is up to you.*

She could have screamed, because *the rest* was a tiger, a lion, and a massive liger, all out for blood.

Goode roared in a *Get her* kind of way, and the trio surged forward.

Jake used his height to swing at them with superhuman strength. Ella was the lowest to the ground, and she used that to her advantage, ducking under the rushing tiger's claws and snapping at his neck. She sank her teeth deep into his flesh and hung on. The tiger shook and roared, trying to claw her off. Screeches filled the air as the owls dive-bombed their foes. Jake grunted and swung the branch, sending the lion flying against a boulder with a bone-crunching thump. Ella darted away from the tiger and circled back to Jake's side.

Keep your back to the tree, she told him in a fox whine.

"Get out of here, Ella. Go," he murmured out of the corner of his mouth.

She swatted his leg with her tail and growled. Like hell, she would.

Goode slunk forward, swiping at Jake with a paw, but Jake batted it away. For a moment, they were at an impasse, both sides staring each other down. The tiger circled one way while

Goode circled the other way. Ella and Jake circled too, communicating wordlessly, forming a team.

Goode flicked his tail and curled his lips into a cruel smile that said, *I will crush you, little one.*

Ella snarled hard enough to make her throat ache. *It's not the size of the dog in the fight. It's the size of the fight in the dog.*

And all of a sudden, she was soaring through the air at the liger, only realizing what had happened a second later. Goode hadn't leaped at her. She'd leaped at him, initiating the next attack. A pang of *oh, shit* terror hit her in midair, but a second later, all she felt was a rush. She'd fought for just causes before, but love superseded all that.

Love makes us stronger, her fox said, aiming for Goode's ear.

Ironic, but true. Ever since she'd met Jake, she'd worried that falling in love would make her weaker. But the opposite was true.

You messed with the wrong fox, Goode, she snarled, sinking her teeth into his fur, hoping Jake would understand her plan. Her teeth wouldn't pierce the liger's thick ruff, but if she dragged his head down to one side. . .

She missed, pivoted, and chomped down on his ear, yanking down with all her might. And, *thwack!* Jake hammered down with his branch, and Goode staggered.

Perfect! she wanted to cheer.

But there wasn't time, because the second she stumbled away, the tiger — Burman — chased her down. He roared, spread his front paws wide, and then smacked them together to trap her. But Jake whacked the tiger's haunches while the owls harried its ears, allowing Ella to make a terrifying, out-of-the-jaws-of-death escape. Terrifying, yet exhilarating at the same time. She turned on the twice-her-size tiger, snapping wildly at its neck. The beast scuttled backward with a *what-the-fuck* look of surprise, and Ella turned back to Jake.

No! she barked as Goode rose on his back legs to tower over Jake. She could see it already — the liger crashing down on her fearless mate, crushing and tearing. Not content with killing Jake but ripping him to shreds.

Jake wielded his branch like a club and sidestepped, motioning toward the house. "Over there!"

She wanted to scream. No, she was not going to make her escape while Jake sacrificed himself. And no, she wasn't going to go after Burman, who was slinking away into the woods. She was going to fight at Jake's side.

"Get it!" he yelled.

She did a double take. Get what?

Goode roared and dove for Jake.

No! she screamed.

"Get it!" Jake yelled, more desperately this time.

His words were so adamant, she looked around, trying to locate what *it* was. The hoe leaning against the side of the house? The chipped flowerpot on the porch?

There. That, her fox cried.

A ray of sunlight angled through the clearing and glinted off a metal blade. The machete left in a stump by the porch.

Ella rushed forward, making the fastest shift of her life. Her four-footed sprint became an upright, human run. Her paws widened into hands. In one furious movement, she yanked the machete free and turned back to the fight.

"Jake!" she yelled, rushing at the faint stripes of Goode's back.

Jake was punching at the liger's muzzle, but the beast had him pinned to the ground. Goode spread his jaws wide. His teeth showed a pure, terrifying white.

"No!" Ella screamed, swinging the machete.

The liger's ear flicked, distracted just long enough for Jake to heave him away. Really *heave* with uncanny strength that sent the beast rolling. Jake followed with his body until man and beast were both tangled and wrestling.

Ella resisted the temptation to chop at the liger's thrashing legs. That wouldn't end this fight. Only a mortal blow would, but Jake was too close to Goode's chest for her to attempt that now.

Jake, she screamed in her mind. *Get clear. I need you to get clear.*

She could picture him giving her that chagrined look he did so well. *I'm trying.*

Goode's claws sliced into Jake's shoulder, and he let out a muffled grunt. One of those tough-soldier cries that hinted he didn't have much left.

"Jake!" she yelled, putting every promise, every hope into her voice. "Now!"

Jake shoved, pushing the liger off-balance. Goode rolled sideways, his chest exposed. Ella dove in the split second she had and stabbed the machete deep into the monster's heart. Goode roared and clawed at her, but Jake wrestled him back.

Twist it, her fox screamed. *Turn the blade.*

Ella wrenched the machete sideways and closed her eyes, hanging on. There was never any satisfaction in killing, not even a beast like Goode. A gruesome death was even worse, the kind likely to haunt her long after the thrashing ceased and the choked pants died out. But there was no other way. Goode had killed ruthlessly before; he would kill again unless she stopped him. So she twisted the blade and held on until Goode bled out past the point shifter healing could repair. Even after his chest fell for the last time and went limp, she hung on, hating what that evil creature had made her do.

For a second, the clearing went totally quiet except for the uncertain *Hoo* of an owl. Then something twitched under her body, and she panicked that Goode wasn't dead.

"Ella." It was Jake, dragging himself out from under the beast and whispering her name.

For the space of three heavy heartbeats, they stared at each other. Then she pulled him clear and smothered him in a hug.

"Jake." She moved her hands helplessly over his body. Blood soaked every inch of his tattered clothes, and her heart cried. Would Jake bleed to death too?

He held her tightly — really tightly, and for a moment, she feared it was the clutch of a dying man. But when his hands moved, it struck her that his muscles were tight with life.

"This is what was keeping us apart?" Jake whispered. Then he grinned wildly, as if he barely felt his injuries, the way she'd seen soldiers get high on the adrenaline rush of a life-or-death fight. "You think I'd let four feet and a tail keep us apart?" He looked down at Goode's lifeless body. "If I'm not hallucinating. Tell me I'm not hallucinating."

She shook her head. "We're shifters, Jake. Goode and his men, too. And not just them. Kai. Hunter..."

His eyes went wide. "Kai is a tiger?"

She gulped. Was Jake ready to hear about dragons? "There are all kinds of shifters. But, Jake, that's not all."

He winced, and she couldn't tell whether his injuries were registering or whether he dreaded whatever she had to say.

"So, tell me," he insisted. "Damn it, Ella. If we can beat this, we can beat anything."

He motioned around, and her stomach roiled. *This* was the shifter fight, and Jake's injuries were deep. Worse, they were inflicted by shifters. A tiny minority of humans wounded by shifters became shifters too, matching their attackers' species.

Her inner fox whimpered. Jake, a liger?

Shit. She hated the idea of Jake turning into the kind of monstrous hybrid Mother Nature had never designed. But that was better than the alternative — death. Most humans died from shifter-inflicted wounds in the same process that killed the majority of human males who mated with shifter females. Their bodies fought the change too much.

She closed her eyes and held Jake tighter, letting the tears flow. How could she tell him? What should she tell him? He seemed so strong now, but shifter essence was already circulating in his bloodstream, ready to get to work.

Mate, her fox whimpered. *My poor mate.*

"Hey," he whispered, stroking her bare skin. "It will be okay."

She shook her head against his uninjured shoulder, smearing it with tears. Her mother's mate, Brian, had said that too.

"Jake," she mumbled, still not knowing what to say.

Something warmed against her hip, and she glanced down.

Jake grimaced and wiggled his hand into his pocket. "I know. That thing burns."

She stared at the little white pouch he withdrew. "What thing?"

"This." He worked the pouch strap loose and pulled something out. "I have no idea why. It didn't feel warm when I found it."

Ella gaped at the smooth, oval stone in his hand. Flecks of blue, red, and green glittered over a black core, like so many jewels all pressed into one.

Like this, Silas had said that day he'd shown her the illustration of the creation of the Spirit Stones. *This is what we're looking for. An opal. The Keystone. The stone with magic powers. The mother of all Spirit Stones.*

She cupped her hand around Jake's, afraid to speak, to touch. Too overwhelmed to think clearly. The opal was hot and throbbing with energy.

Throbbing with power, her fox said.

"It's weird, but I felt like it was giving me strength. See?" Jake said, rolling it into her hand.

The second he did, a surge of energy electrified her body, but Jake collapsed at the same time.

"Jake!" she cried.

His eyes rolled back, and his hands shook. His voice became a hoarse whisper, his face, ash-white. "Ella... Love... you..."

"Jake!" For one terrifying moment, all she could do was hold him.

Give it back to him. Give it back, quick! her fox screamed.

She shoved the opal into his palm and squeezed it closed. "Can you feel that? Tell me you feel that. Jake, please..."

His blue eyes dimmed, then slid shut, and he went deathly still.

"No..." Ella fought back her rising panic and held his hand in both of hers, keeping the opal tight in his fist. "Please," she whispered. Not to Jake, but to the gem. "Please protect him."

Spirit Stones were supposed to have incredible powers, right?

"Get to work, damn it!" she screamed at the gem.

166

The deepest, faintest bass she'd ever heard whispered in her mind. *I have great power. But those wounds are severe. If this warrior is to live, he must summon the power within him. You must do the same.*

She nestled close, pushing her remaining energy into Jake — every last scrap she had with every breath she took. She closed her eyes and thought of all the experiences they had shared — all the *I can't haves*, all the *shouldn'ts*. For months, frustration had eaten away at her, but now, she let it fuel her anger and determination to hang on.

Destiny, you are a bitch, she wanted to scream.

The ancient voice tut-tutted in her mind. *Destiny rewards the worthy.*

Jake is worthy! she snapped.

There was no answer, just a grim silence that said more than words. *He is worthy. Are you?*

Ella hugged Jake, keeping the opal tight in his hands. Wishing another couple of tigers would come prowling out of the underbrush so she could lash out in rage. Destiny wanted her to prove herself? Fine. She would.

But there was no foe to outfox, no battle but the one within. And then it hit her. She had to prove her love, not her fighting prowess. But how? She loved Jake with all her heart. She always had.

We rejected him too, her fox cried, ashamed.

That was for his own protection!

Protecting him or protecting yourself? her fox whined.

The thought knocked her back on her heels. Hadn't she loved Jake unconditionally?

You wanted him unconditionally, but that isn't the same thing.

She squeezed her eyes shut, trying to push the pain away until it dawned on her. Maybe that was her problem. Maybe pain was part of love, and she had to accept that.

But I don't want to accept that, she wanted to yell. *Why would love be intertwined with sorrow?*

Her mind raced over the past year and a half. Every time they'd parted, it had been at her insistence. Jake was the one who'd looked at her with puppy dog eyes that said, *I believe.*

Did she believe too?

Of course, I believe, she wanted to say.

Then show it, her fox urged.

But, shit. She hadn't shown emotion to anyone in years. A woman who worked in the toughest military corps didn't do emotion, and she couldn't just turn it on like a switch.

The owls fluttered in the trees, and one hooted sadly, bringing her further back in time. Back to her teenage years, when she'd lived on this plot of land with her foster brothers and Georgia Mae. Even back then, she'd put up an emotional wall. She'd played rough and tough to keep up with Hunter and Kai, insisting to Georgia Mae she didn't need any girl talks and that she didn't need to talk about her mom.

A hard lump rose in her throat. Her mother had loved and lost; Ella feared the same fate. So she shuttered herself off from love and pushed Jake away.

She squeezed her eyes shut and hugged him tighter, trying to unlock that hidden place in her soul.

"Please," she whispered, as much to Jake as to herself. "Please."

Slowly, tears started to trickle out. Tears she'd never shown anyone. She brushed her cheek against his shoulder, rubbing the drops into his skin.

"I love you," she whispered, clutching him as the ache in her heart ballooned.

Embrace it, the Keystone whispered. *Pain is love.*

She thought of Jake lying in bed the previous night, quietly studying her, stroking her skin. His blue eyes shone with a mixture of sadness and hope — the bravest combination of all. She thought of him clearing his throat that day on the porch and quietly asking, *What is it, Ella? What's keeping us apart?*

Courage. The man had it in droves. The kind of courage needed to face a powerful enemy — and the kind of courage that let a man put his heart out on a limb.

The tears came faster, freer as she found the courage too. The courage to face loving Jake with everything that involved — highs, lows, compromises. Worst of all, loss.

"I love you," she whispered. "I'll always love you."

She gathered up her sorrow like so many flowers in a wilted bouquet. Then she cried. Sobbed, really, because this was it. This was exactly what her mother must have gone through. The emptiness, the sorrow. The soul-draining despair. The never-ending inner chant of *please, please, please* while a tiny ray of hope flickered uncertainly.

Jake lay perfectly still, barely breathing. Dying?

Please, she cried. *Please, not him.*

She kept the *don't let me lose him* part out of her silent prayers, because this wasn't about her happiness. It was about the life of an honest, honorable man.

Please. Please let him live.

Heat poured from the gem — heat and energy so intense, she could feel it through Jake's hand.

Please...

The heat intensified to a near burn, and suddenly, Jake sucked in a deep breath. His exhale was rattly, but the next inhale was smoother, and the other one after that, too.

"Jake," she whispered, not daring to hope.

His eyes fluttered open, glazed over at first, then slowly clearing as he focused on her then looked at his hand in wonder.

"Maybe I should hang on to this for a while longer," he muttered in a hoarse voice. Then his eyes slid shut, but his chest continued to rise and fall.

"You are definitely hanging on to it," Ella said, trying to be strong but failing utterly. Mumbling a thousand thanks in her mind. So what if the ordeal turned Jake into a tiger, lion, or even a liger? Jake was Jake, and she would celebrate his survival for the rest of her life.

Just think, her fox whispered. *If the Keystone protects him through this change, it will protect him through a mating bite.*

Ella's eyes snapped open as her inner fox wagged its tail wildly. Could it be true?

Silly fox, she chastised a moment later, catching herself. Poor Jake was covered in blood and wounds. He'd had the worst possible introduction to the shifter world. This wasn't the time to think of such things.

Jake pulled himself to a seated position despite her protests. "Um, Ella?"

She gulped down the lump in her throat and waited for more.

"You're... kind of... naked." He pointed out.

She pulled him into a huge hug. Yes, there was a lot she had to explain to him about the shifter world.

"Seems I can't help it around you," she said, wiping her tears.

"Can't say I mind—" Jake started, then went stiff as he stared behind her.

She whirled as a growl sounded in her ears. The lion was back and stalking toward them with a slight limp, its eyes red with revenge. Behind him, the bushes rustled. Was that the tiger coming back too?

"Shit." Ella jumped to her feet and looked around. The machete was too far to reach. She'd have no choice but to shift, and that lion was three times her size. Jake would try to help, which meant he would reopen his wounds — at best. At worst...

You will die, the lion's growl said.

Ella clenched her fists, preparing to shift. No way was she losing this battle now.

Then, out of nowhere, the sound of tires crunching over gravel reached her ears, and she snapped her head around, expecting to see a vehicle. But the heavy footsteps of some huge beast preceded it, and she caught sight of a huge, brown blur approaching through the trees.

Ella stepped back, protecting Jake. "God, not more shifters now..."

Jake struggled to his feet and swayed, one hand tight around the opal. "More of Goode's men?"

A massive grizzly hurtled into view, barreling straight for the lion.

"Hunter!" Her voice shook with relief.

The lion snarled in surprise and fled into the woods with Hunter hot on its heels. The tiger was out there somewhere as well, but the shaking bushes indicated he, too, was fleeing for his life.

"Hunter?" Jake murmured, his jaw hanging open. "Shit, there are more," he muttered when two tigers sprinted through the clearing, racing after the others.

Ella shook her head. "It's all right. That's Cruz and Jody."

A Land Rover screeched to a halt by the gate, and Kai jumped out. "Sorry," he called as he raced over to Ella. "I would have flown over, but I couldn't risk it in daylight."

"Tell me he means flying in the helicopter," Jake murmured.

Ella decided to let the dragon part slide for now.

"You okay, Jake?" Kai called.

Jake nodded weakly. "A little confused. . . but okay. What about Nina?"

Ella melted all over again. Leave it to Jake to consider another person at a time like that.

Kai grinned. "Doing great, from what I hear. The twins too. It's Boone who nearly passed out."

As he spoke, Kai pulled his shirt off and handed it to Ella. Seeing each other naked was all par for the course with shifters, but still, she was happy to cover up. Being naked was a lot more fun with just Jake around.

"So, how many others? Where?" Kai demanded, scowling at Goode's body.

Ella pointed into the woods. "One lion, one tig—"

She'd barely finished the word when a bloodcurdling feline scream sounded from the woods.

"Make that just one lion," Kai murmured.

The undergrowth thrashed, and a series of heated growls ensued. Then came a piercing roar, another scream, and after that, the forest stilled.

Ella clutched Jake's hand, watching the woods for some sign. Finally, Hunter, Jody, and Cruz strode back into the clearing, and she exhaled.

"Thank goodness."

Jake tugged her hand. "Please tell me they're the good guys."

"They're the good guys," Ella assured him, happier than ever to see her friends.

Cruz and Jody, the tigers, turned and rubbed their bodies together in long, comforting strokes that started at the nose and ended at the tail. Hunter prowled around the perimeter of the property, muttering to himself in bear talk.

Ella gently steered Jake to sit on the stairs and crouched in front of him. "Are you sure you're all right?"

He nodded, looking more shell-shocked than anything else.

Jesus, how did he survive that? Kai murmured into Ella's mind in a low, concerned voice as the others edged forward, still in animal form.

She held Jake's hands tightly, assuring herself he was okay. Then she made space for the others to see and nodded to Jake. "Show them. Just don't let go."

The right side of his mouth curled up. "Believe me, I plan to hang on to this for a while." He opened his cupped hands just enough to reveal the opal.

The sun glinted off its mottled surface, sending out rays of multicolored light.

"Holy shit." Kai stepped back.

Cruz gave a surprised growl, and Hunter chuffed.

Jake shot a pointed look around the animals who'd stalked across the yard to inspect him. "You can say that again."

Chapter Seventeen

One week later...

For the next week, Jake drifted in and out of dreams. Good dreams. Ugly dreams. Confusing dreams too. And the most unsettling part? Some of them may not have been dreams at all.

There were the feverish dreams where he sweated buckets and fought death away — not on a field of battle but in a bed. A good thing Ella was there, keeping him from drifting off into the pit of darkness that seemed intent on swallowing him up. The opal was in his hand, too, helping him fight the fever with its own piercing heat. He spent a lot of time lying motionless while a whirlwind churned inside him. A battle that pitted his body against... something else. Something dangerous, yet enticing. Totally unfamiliar, yet natural at the same time.

"Ella," he whispered from time to time, waiting for the squeeze of her hand that said, *I'm right here. Not going anywhere, McBride.*

Eventually, death went from crowding his space to creeping all the way over to the edge of the room until it finally threw in the towel and disappeared. The fever broke, and his dreams became pleasant fantasies — like him touching Ella, or Ella touching him. Make that, Ella doing a hell of a lot more than touching him, which felt so, so good. They talked in those fantasies, and that was nice even if Ella sounded a lot more conflicted than he wanted her to be.

Jake, you'll be a shifter too.

A shifter. That sounded cool. He liked that dream.

A fox, like you. He'd nodded and smiled like it was the most normal thing.

You might come out differently, she'd said in a strangely choked voice. *You could be a liger like Gideon.*

He remembered shaking his head firmly. *I want to be a fox like you.*

Foxes were tough and agile and resourceful. Foxes roamed the mountains, totally free.

Ella had gulped and gone quiet for a while before whispering, *I'd have to bite you before your injuries make you a liger.*

So, bite me, he remembered saying — or dreaming — without considering anything other than *Ella. Me. Together.* Whatever it took.

It shouldn't be like this, Ella had cried — really cried — when she leaned over his neck and touched him. *It should be good.*

This is good, he'd assured her, and that was the truth. Her body, so close to his. Her lips on his skin. Even the scrape of her teeth felt good. There was the briefest pinch of pain before a hot, piercing surge zipped through his veins like lightning, turning on every switch in him. *Really* turned on in a way that felt so good, he ended up tugging Ella into a straddle over him, cowgirl style. Before long, she was moaning and rocking, and he was thrusting, filled with inexplicable energy and desire. And when she sank her teeth into his neck for a second time, he'd exploded inside her and howled with the pleasure of it all.

So — dream? Fantasy? Jake would have sworn it was the former if it weren't for the tiny scars on his neck. The barely there marks he kept touching and wondering about.

All that had wiped him out for the next few days, and he'd fallen into a deep, easy sleep. No more nightmares. No more fever. No need to hang on to that opal all the time, because his body was healing on its own for a change. Whenever he woke, Ella was nestled alongside him, refusing to let go.

And finally, a few days later, he awoke totally clear-headed and alert for the first time. He cracked his eyes open without moving, just in case. Where was he? Was everything really okay?

He exhaled a moment later, because Ella was spooned along the curve of his chest, asleep. The light pouring through the big windows was the saturated pink of daybreak, and he and Ella were in a creaky bed. The one in her room at one end of the plantation house at Koakea, it seemed. Slowly, he raised his right hand and studied it, front and back. Then he clenched it a few times, checking the shape. He'd had some weird dreams in which his fists had been more like paws with tufts of coppery fur, and he and Ella had been running — no, scampering — over a western landscape, both of them on four feet, swishing their tails.

He opened and closed his fist. Was he really turning part animal, or was he just going nuts?

A faint, barking laugh sounded somewhere deep inside his soul and whispered so quietly, he had to strain to hear. *Not going nuts. Just finding me.*

Finding who?

Me. You. We're the same.

The curtains rustled in a light breeze, and trees swayed outside the window, giving him a glimpse of the moon sliding toward the western horizon. Which confirmed how much time had gone by, because the last he remembered, the moon had been a lot thinner than that. Something swelled in his chest, and he found himself humming. Why, he couldn't tell. Only that it felt good. He hummed a little more, trying to find a tune that sounded right. Eventually, he settled on a long, low note, a little like a howl.

Which probably meant he was going crazy. But, wow. He hadn't felt that settled, that peaceful in years. Like he had somehow fast-forwarded through a decade and finally put his inner demons to rest. Even when the moon slipped out of sight, he could feel its comforting gravity out there.

"Mmm," Ella mumbled, shifting in his arms.

Jake nuzzled her shoulder, sniffing deeply. Ella's desert rose scent seemed richer, more intense than before, as did the fragrance of tropical flowers drifting in through the open windows.

The salt air tickled his nose, and his ears picked up the faintest sounds — not just the brush of tree branches over the roof but the scratchy movement of insects outside.

"Perfect morning," Ella mumbled.

Perfect for a run, that inner voice said.

Which was ridiculous. Why run when he could lounge in bed with the woman of his dreams?

Why lounge when we can run with the woman of our dreams? the voice retorted.

"You okay?" Ella whispered.

He nodded slowly. "Just trying to figure out what parts are real and what parts are a dream."

She kissed his knuckles. Her brow was knotted, her lips tight. "Shifters are real. It's all real, Jake."

He held her hands again. "So... you can change back and forth. Like at the full moon?"

The deep, inner voice scoffed. *Of course not.*

"*You* can change back and forth," Ella said. "Well, you'll be able to soon. Whenever you want. It doesn't depend on the moon."

He looked out the window. Funny, he could swear he could feel it out there. Calling to him like an irresistible siren, begging him to come outside and play.

"The moon does guide us sometimes," she added, following his eyes. "In subtle ways — the same way it affects humans, I suppose."

"And the bite part?" He touched his neck. The scars acted like an *on* switch for lust, and he started nuzzling Ella all over again. Up and down her neck, then down to her chest, making him crazy with desire.

Mark her, the inner voice growled. *Make her ours.*

"The bite makes us mates," she sighed, lying back, letting him explore. "Bound forever. I hope you're okay with that."

He chuckled against her skin. Hell yeah, he was okay with that. "I just wish we could do it again."

Ella flashed a sultry smile. "Good thing we can. Anytime you want. You owe me a bite, McBride. That will complete the rite. It will complete us."

His pulse shot through the roof, and his eyebrows jumped up. "I like the sound of that. But it is a little intimidating. What if I mess up?"

She smiled. "If you listen to instinct, you can't go wrong."

Instinct, huh? Was that the voice he'd been hearing?

"When?" he whispered.

"Whenever you want. Whenever you're ready. The best thing is, we can do it again and again."

It should have sounded terrifying, but he was strangely tempted — and totally turned on. "So, kind of like marriage on overdrive?" he joked.

Ella shook her head and cupped his cheeks, looking deep into his eyes. "Mating is more than that, Jake. It's more than a promise or a piece of paper. It's forever — really forever."

He grinned. "Some forevers, I wouldn't want. But forever with you? Yes, please."

She snuggled against his chest again, exuding warmth and relief. "There's so much I have to explain."

"I guess so. But one thing at a time is plenty for me. And I'm happy to start with the forever part."

He nuzzled her a little longer, tempted to get down to loving Ella. After all, if she was his, they could make love as often as they liked, and he had a lot to make up for. But the urge to run grew even stronger, making it impossible to ignore. He sat up slowly, carefully, surprised not to feel too sore.

Not sore. Need to move. To shift.

"Jake?" Ella sat up, touching his thigh.

He wanted to stop and kiss her. To thread his fingers through her hair and spend another hour kissing that gloriously naked flesh. But the instinct to move grew ever more urgent, so he lowered his feet to the floor.

"Just a second," he murmured, not sure what instinct he was following, only that he had to follow it right away.

He padded toward the door and out onto the long front porch, confused. Why did his body feel so surprisingly good, yet so achy at the same time?

"You okay?" Ella's voice drifted after him.

He nodded, hating to leave her behind but desperate to dig his bare toes into the earth too. The need was so intense that even after he descended the porch stairs and felt the moist soil under his feet, he needed more.

Keep going. Sniff. Run. Roll, the inner voice urged.

His back went from feeling fine to incredibly stiff until he hunched over, which was better.

"Jake!" Ella called, running to his side.

He wanted to turn and assure her it was okay. Instead, he fell to his knees and propped himself up with his arms. Not collapsing, just...

Shifting, the hoarse voice inside him urged. *Let me out.*

"Jake," Ella cried, running her hands over his back.

Mmm. Nice, the voice hummed.

It was nice. He closed his eyes and tucked his chin against his chest, moving under her hand.

"Whoa. Already?" Ella murmured.

Jake had no idea what was going on. But he was tired of resisting whatever that was inside his body. He breathed deeply, consuming a whole new world of scents and sounds.

Ella kept right on petting him, which was good, because every joint suddenly ached, and his skin itched like hell.

"Show me, my mate," she whispered.

Show her what? How crazy he was?

Show her me, the inner voice hissed.

"It only hurts for a second," Ella said, though her voice sounded far away.

He grunted, because it did hurt. But, like Ella said, just for one blinding second. Then all he felt was the crazy-good sensation of Ella's fingers over his back.

"Wow. Jake," she whispered.

He still had his eyes closed, but *wow* was right. He smelled flowers and grass, layers deep. Nice, rich earth under his four feet, perfect for digging his claws into...

His mind spun. Whoa. How many feet?

But Ella kept right on petting him. "You did it, Jake. Look."

He blinked a few times, then sneezed. The color had seeped out of the tropical landscape, and little ribbons of shadow moved when he moved his head.

Ella laughed and stroked his ears. Ears that stuck up from the top, not the sides of his head. "Come on, look."

He cocked his head at her then froze. His nose was way out in front of his head. The tip was dark, and whiskers stuck out on both sides.

"Most handsome fox ever." Ella grinned.

Most handsome *what?* He wanted to yell, but all that came out was a surprised bark.

"See?" she offered, holding his tail to one side.

Jake stood perfectly still. A tail? Since when?

Shifters are real. It's all real, Jake, Ella had said.

It was one thing to hear someone say it. But to experience it — holy crap.

Ella fell over him in a huge, happy hug. Laughing? Crying? He wanted to hug her back, but he settled for licking her ear with a frighteningly long tongue. The more his tail wagged, the more his hips wiggled, and he twisted around for a look. Wow. He really did have a tail.

"You're just the way I dreamed," Ella mumbled into his fur.

Apparently, she'd dreamed of something that looked a lot like a wolf, but with a fluffier tail and redder fur, if he read the grayscale correctly. As big as a wolf too — and a big wolf, at that — but with a narrower nose. He blinked a few times.

Not a wolf. A fox, stupid, the voice snarled.

He turned and nearly tripped over his own feet. Which one was he supposed to move first?

Ella grinned a mile wide. "Hang on. I'll show you."

A second later, she hunched over and shifted. A smooth, easy shift in which her human features gradually blurred and gave way to a sleek, furry body and a joyous, thumping tail.

Ella, he said in surprise, which came out as a yip.

She yipped back, and they stood there for a moment, two foxes, nose-to-nose. Her eyes were bright, her nose twitching.

Without even thinking about it, he started circling her, sniffing every inch of her body. And, wow — he could smell the excitement in her. The joy. Even a hint of desire. And best of all, he smelled himself on her — and her on him.

Mate, the deep, inner voice rumbled. *My mate.*

He wanted to rub against her. Lick her. Romp around the plantation with her. He wanted everything at once, but hell, he could barely coordinate his feet.

Ella broke out in happy yips and danced around him in delight. So joyous and excited, he started lumbering around too.

A fox! You're a fox! Her voice echoed in his mind.

Ella's orange-brown eyes shone, and her fur glinted in the morning sun in exactly the same way her human hair usually did. She tilted her head the same way too. So Ella was Ella — trim, petite, and beautiful — while he was a darker, XXL version of her. He turned a few circles, trying to get a look at himself and nearly tripping over his own feet. Boy, did he have a lot to learn.

Come on! Ella bounded away like it was all so easy. As easy as it was for his mind to translate her yips into words. Which — whoa — hit him a second later. How the heck did that work?

Can you hear me? He tried pushing his thoughts into her mind.

Of course I can.

He snorted. Of course. This was going to take some getting used to, for sure.

He took one wobbly step then another while Ella trotted around him in circles, brushing against his fur.

Nothing to it, she hummed, winding around his body a second time.

The more she touched him — distracting him, tempting him — the less he thought about the mechanics of walking, and the more smoothly he moved. Before long, he was trotting along, ducking under branches that tickled his back and sneezing away the pungent scent of exotic flowers.

Time to hustle, soldier, Ella teased, racing off.

Get her, the inner voice urged him. *Catch our mate.*

He shot off in pursuit, intent on catching up but distracted at the same time. Was his tongue supposed to hang out the side of his mouth, or did it belong straight down the middle? Was his tail too high or too low?

Whatever, the inner voice said. *Just run.*

So he pounded the dirt, chasing his mate. Once he got the hang of the four-legged gait, he had the raw speed to catch Ella. But she was agile as anything, and every time he got within an inch of her tail, she'd dodge away with a lightning move he could barely follow. But it was fun — the kind of flat-out, panting, childish fun he hadn't experienced in years. The plantation grounds he'd patrolled so often became a playground, full of joy and wonder. The rich, moist soil. The scratchy blades of native grass. The overgrown taro patch he and Ella splashed through. So many details he had never picked up on before came alive. How had he missed so much?

Then he skidded to a stop, growling, every hair on his body bristling. Something was wrong. Very wrong.

What is it? Ella asked, looping around to stand beside him.

He sidestepped, trying to keep his body between Ella and the intruder he sensed. Then he sniffed and pawed the ground, trying to place the scent.

Ella sniffed the spot at his feet then laughed. *That's just Boone.*

Jake went right on growling. Boone was a great guy, but the idea of a male wolf infringing on Jake's home turf activated overprotective instincts to the max.

Ella wound her body around his, reassuring him with a chattering sound. *You know the guys as well as I do. They're okay.*

He kept right on snarling under his breath. Any other guy close to his mate was *not* okay.

Must finish the mating process. Must make her ours, his fox growled in his mind.

The bite mark on his neck itched, and he stared at Ella. She did say he owed her a bite, so maybe...

181

Whenever you want, she'd said. *Whenever you're ready. If you listen to instinct, you can't go wrong.*

And damn, did he feel ready. Desperately ready.

Bite her. Complete the rite, the inner voice said. *Safer that way,* that inner voice said.

Bite to the neck and *safe* didn't sound like two things that fit together, and yet his body heated with the idea.

Ella swung her head west. *That patch of woods over there is full of bear scent, and over on the other side of Koa Point, you'll smell tiger. This is their home, after all. Are you getting all possessive on me?*

He sidled closer and rubbed his neck against hers. *Not sure I can help it.*

Part of him rebelled against the idea. A woman wasn't an object to be possessed — especially a woman like Ella. But another part of him — the fox, no doubt — was totally enamored of the idea.

She can be ours forever. No one could force us apart.

Jake liked that part. And Ella had bitten him, which meant she was okay with the *forever* part, right?

Ella flicked her tail and bounced away. *If you want me, you have to catch me,* she teased, speeding off again.

Jake flicked his tail — a simple move, yet one he was ridiculously proud of pulling off — and sprinted after her. This time, she wasn't getting away.

Just leave the running to me, his fox side rumbled.

Jake had to admit that made more sense than him tripping over his own feet. Someday, he'd master the four-footed thing. Right now, all that mattered was his mate.

His paws hammered over the ground. Branches swatted his shoulders. Ella's tail waved like a flag as she led him on a wild chase across the plantation grounds. Twice, he drew close enough to pounce, but each time, she darted away, laughing.

Beat you to the water, Ella teased as she sprinted toward the beach.

Jake gritted his teeth and swallowed his reply. No, she wouldn't beat him. Not if he could help it. He raced on, closing the distance between them by the time Ella reached the rocky rise that hemmed in the beach.

Now! he yelled at his fox side, timing his leap.

Ella dodged to the right as he anticipated, and he caught her with a flying tackle. A second later, they tumbled to the ground. He came out on top, panting wildly.

Gotcha!

Got her, his fox agreed with a happy yip.

Oh, you think so? Ella said, looking coy. *What if I do this?*

She squirmed a little, and the air around her shimmered. In a flash, she shifted to human form right under him. Then she lay back, naked, watching him with eyes that glinted with some secret plan.

Jake froze, unsure what to do.

Time for you to take over, his fox said. *Just make sure you listen when it comes to the bite.*

Shifting back to human form happened so fast, Jake didn't realize it was happening until he came down over Ella on his elbows and knees. He lowered himself until his chest pressed down on hers. Her eyes were bright with lust and love, and the only move she made was to shift her legs to give him more space.

"Gotcha," he said in a husky voice.

"Got me." Her eyes weren't just sparkling. They were glowing. "Not bad for your first time, McBride."

First time implied more occasions when they might engage in this kind of fun. If he'd still had a tail, he would have wagged it wildly.

The palm trees overhead swayed, tossing shadows over their bodies. The fine layer of sand they'd landed in formed a firm mattress for their bodies, and the wind whispered through the fronds above.

"I think you let me catch you, Kitt."

"Oh, I would never do such a thing." She ran her heel along his leg, sending spears of heat through his veins. "Then where would we be?"

He chuckled. "How about naked and alone on the beach?"

Ella tucked her chin and looked down at their bodies. "Hmm. Naked and alone. Now what?"

He grinned and shifted his weight, letting her feel the hard prod of his cock. "I have an idea."

"And what would that be, soldier?" She stretched her arms over her head and crooked an eyebrow. Her scent wrapped around him, thick with lust.

"I was thinking about kissing. Touching," he murmured, letting his lips play over her collarbone.

"Sounds so tame," Ella said, though her body arched under his, inviting him to explore.

He slid his right hand along her body. Slow and gentle over the swell of her breast on the way down, heavier on the way up. Then he kissed her, and she kissed back, hard. After sweeping his tongue over hers, he pulled away long enough to pant, "I can pretty much guarantee this isn't going to be tame."

"Good." She hauled him into another deep, hungry kiss.

The air grew thick with a sticky-sweet scent that could only be lust, and Ella's body surged under his. Her legs hugged his waist. He swept his thumb over her nipple, making it peak.

Soon, the inner voice whispered as he slid over her body, gathering the flesh of her breast with his hand. He suckled harder until Ella whimpered in need.

"Yes..." she murmured, threading her fingers through his hair.

She tasted so good. Felt so good. Sounded so good.

Mine, his fox howled. *Mine.*

He worked his hand lower, closing in on her wet heat. His finger slipped straight through her folds. Then he reached deeper and circled inside, making her moan.

"Yes..."

Never had he gone so quickly from *tempted* to blind, raging need. Never had he sensed such an urgency to bond.

Make her ours. Forever, the voice inside screamed.

He nipped her breast then moved back to her neck, homing in on the spot that called to him.

"Yes," Ella whispered. "Right there."

He scraped his teeth over her skin, and she surged against him.

"Do it. Please. I trust you." She tilted her head, giving him a glimpse of her neck.

Jake pushed her legs wider with a knee, positioning himself at her entrance, letting instinct take over.

I got this, his fox assured him. *But first, you have to—*

He rolled his hips, plunging deep, making Ella cry out in ecstasy.

Yeah, he knew what came first, all right. Hot, raging sex with the woman he loved.

I got this, he muttered. This part, he didn't need any help with. He pulled out, aching all over, then slid back in.

Ella gasped, clamping her legs around him, telling him how good she felt.

Out and in, out and in. He settled into a barely controlled rhythm, watching Ella without really watching, because the sensation was so intense. The waves rolling over sand not far behind him urged him on as fiercely as Ella did with her hands and voice.

"Harder. Please. Harder..."

He pulled her leg higher against his side and thrust deeper still, slowing down to relish every hot, tight inch.

There, his fox urged, pulling his attention back to her neck.

Everything narrowed to a tunnel of vision focused entirely on the notch at the side of her throat, and he started suckling her skin.

"Yes..." she moaned, guiding him a little higher.

His gums grew hot and his canines extended, but somehow, that didn't alarm him. In fact, it felt good in the same way his cock felt good pushing through the tight grip of Ella's inner muscles. And when he scraped his teeth over her neck for a second time, his body flared with primal need.

There. Bite deep. Mark her as yours, the voice inside him urged.

"Jake..." Ella moaned.

Her body tensed all over as she raced toward a powerful orgasm. He withdrew, paused, then thrust back in, giving her what she needed. Once, twice—

"Yes!" Ella cried as her body shuddered into a high.

The moment Jake exploded into his own orgasm, he plunged his teeth into her neck. A blinding white light erased everything but the feel of their straining bodies and the faint bump of Ella's pulse near his teeth.

Hold on. Keep your lips sealed, an inner voice ordered.

Orders Jake followed very carefully because, holy shit. Was he really doing this?

Just hang on. Bite deeper, the voice said. *Let it feel good.*

He did as he was told, relishing the incredible high. Ella writhed in ecstasy, and his body felt electrified. Alive with pleasure.

He hung on and on, barely noticing when the climax became a heady afterglow. Long after his teeth receded, he kept his lips in a tight seal.

"Oh, yes..." Ella groaned, tensing with a final aftershock of pleasure, then going limp.

Jake pressed his tongue over the bite marks, making sure the wounds had sealed before he let go and dropped to her chest, gasping. He had to be crushing Ella, but she didn't seem to mind.

Definitely don't mind, she murmured, reading his thoughts. She ran her hands over his back and made a low, cooing sound like a bird content with its nest.

Mine, Jake's fox growled.

"Mine," he panted into her neck. His old life seemed a million miles away, and a bright future beckoned with glimpses of the kind of life he'd barely allowed himself to dream of. A lifetime spent with Ella, together. Forever.

"Mine," she agreed, hugging him with her arms and legs. "Forever."

Chapter Eighteen

"How do I look?" Ella asked, turning to Jake three days later.

He had that goofy, *You always look great* expression, which didn't help at all — other than making her feel like a million bucks. Then his eyes flashed, showing his inner fox, who growled, *You look like mine.*

And you're mine, her fox side practically purred in reply.

It was amazing the way a few days — even a few minutes — could change a woman's life. Jake had survived the fight and the change that had made him a shifter. He'd recovered completely and taken quickly to shifting — into a fox, no less. Of course, she would have loved Jake regardless of his animal form, but having him be a fox was just the icing on the cake. She'd lived most of her life among other shifter species, so it felt extra special to finally have someone of her own kind. They could run together, play-hunt together, and explore together, sensing the world in the same way.

"You look nice," Jake said quietly.

Good old Jake, who'd always understood her better than anyone. He knew she didn't feel comfortable with lavish praise — or with things like pretty dresses, like the one she wore now. The yellow one Lily had insisted on during their shopping spree.

Jake was also wearing the spoils of their honeymooner gig — casual, sand-colored slacks that hinted at his perfect ass and a blue polo shirt that stretched nicely over his chest. She swore the man had been a cover model in a previous life.

"Well, you look great," she replied.

Jake looked down at himself, and a glimpse of the country boy showed as he shifted from foot to foot. "Good enough for a wedding?"

"They said casual." She chuckled and stepped closer, fingering his collar as she whispered in his ear. "You look good enough to eat — or strip on the spot and screw."

And man, was she tempted, but she'd already done that earlier that day. Mating had increased their insatiable appetite for sex, and they had been indulging in long, satisfying bouts of sex at all hours of the day. A good thing they weren't on active security duty any more.

"Sounds good to me." Jake's voice was husky as he ran his fingers along her ribs, nearly tickling her breast.

Her inner fox yowled. *Sounds good to me too.*

Ella stopped short of winding her leg around Jake's and slowly pried herself away. "Shoot. We can't be late."

"Oh, right." Jake blinked a few times, pushing back his animal side. "I can't believe Silas and Cassandra put off their wedding for us. But I guess after all the excitement, and the babies..."

She took his hand and led him down the stairs of the plantation house, heading for the winding path to Koa Point. "That's how a pack works." Then she laughed. "Or how a clan works, or a pride, or whatever you choose to call it."

Jake shook his head. "Someday I'll remember which word goes with which species."

Ella laughed. That was the nice thing about Koa Point — the mix of shifters, each ribbing the other about what they ought to call their eclectic little bunch. "Whatever you call it, we're closer than most families."

Jake nodded readily, and she could see the images running through his mind. Shifter packs had a lot in common with military units. "That, I get," he said, then sighed. "But there's a lot I have to learn."

She slid a hand around his waist and into his rear pocket. "Gonna be fun teaching you."

He grinned and put his arm across her shoulders. "Gonna be fun learning."

It was another one of those *pinch me, I'm dreaming moments,* and Ella looked up at the sky. So blue. So perfect.

More perfect than she'd ever dared dream. She was snuggled close to her destined mate, who'd never seemed so lighthearted and relaxed as he did now. Of course, it would be a while until Jake came to terms with all his demons, but he was definitely on his way.

We're on our way, her fox said, and they wound down the path to help their closest friends celebrate a joyous day.

Joyous was right — in more ways than one.

The sound of a baby's cries drifted through the air once Ella and Jake covered the quarter-mile distance to Koa Point and approached the meeting house. Apparently, one of the twins had just woken up. The baby stopped a moment later, soothed by a low hum.

Ella hid a laugh as they came out into the open. "Boone the dad," she whispered to Jake. "Who'd have figured?"

She motioned to where Boone was pacing along the edge of the meeting house, patting a tiny pink bundle on his shoulder, humming to it. Keiki followed closely, jumping at the trailing edge of the baby blanket.

Jake smiled. "I guess people change when the time is right."

Ella looked down at her dress and then at her hand, still clasped in Jake's. Maybe people didn't change so much as let a little of their hidden sides show through.

All for the better, her fox assured her.

Kai looked up and waved. "Ah, so you two finally rolled out of bed long enough to join us, huh?"

Tessa play-smacked her mate before Ella did and stuck her hands on her hips. "I seem to remember a certain dragon lounging around in bed this morning. What was it he said? Oh, yes." Tessa dropped her voice to mimic Kai's. "'Baby, we have plenty of time.'"

"I remember those days," Boone pretended to sigh.

"Right. Like you're hating fatherhood so much," Ella said.

Boone grinned ear to ear and held out little Luna for Ella to admire. "Isn't she something?"

He'd been diapering, burping, and cuddling his twins with gusto over the past week, barely allowing the others to enjoy their new roles as uncles and aunts. Even waking up throughout the night didn't seem to faze Boone.

"She's beautiful," Ella agreed, though all she could see in that swaddle was a tiny little nose. Then she went over to Nina who was sitting on the couch with Kale, the other twin. "How are you doing?"

"Great." Nina beamed. "I'm still sorry about the timing, but I'm doing great. And so is this little guy." She shifted the edge of the blue blanket to reveal her son.

Ella's heart melted all over again. "So cute."

When Ella put her pinkie in his little fist, it looked giant compared to those tiny digits.

"Too bad about the Ferrari, man," Kai teased. "No space for the babies. You're Mr. Minivan now."

Boone shrugged. "We got the Ferrari of minivans."

Ella laughed. Boone's new minivan was red, but that was about all it had in common with the Ferrari.

Baby Kale cried out, and Boone instantly trotted over to swap his daughter for his son.

"I swear you're going to spoil them," Nina said, not managing to sound stern.

"Not possible," Boone insisted. "Not with my babies."

"Well, Auntie Tessa is planning to spoil them the second Boone gives me a chance," Tessa announced. She stayed close to Kai, giving her mate a quick, secret glance that Ella caught. The kind of glance that said, *Watch out, honey. We're next.*

Kai ran his hand over Tessa's back and winked at her, his eyes shining in agreement.

Ella looked around. In some ways, her rough, tough Special Forces comrades hadn't changed a bit. They still ribbed each other mercilessly, made wisecracks, and had their moments of puffing out their chests. In other ways, though, they'd grown up — a lot. They cherished their mates and let tender comments slip — in public, no less. They spoiled Keiki rotten and vied for a chance to hold the babies as much as the women of Koa Point did. But there was more to their subtle transformation than that, though she struggled to find a term for it.

They're settled. Happy. Calm, her fox chipped in. *Civilian, almost.*

That was it. They'd learned to switch on and off their ever-alert soldier sides and enjoy life.

She took Jake's hand and held it close. Jake had come a long way as well. So, someday... Well, who knew? Maybe he would achieve that inner calm too.

Jake brushed his lips over her cheek, and a voice murmured in the back of her mind. The voice of destiny, ancient and wise.

Both of you will.

Me? She wanted to protest. She wasn't the one who'd been casting around for something to do or a place to call home.

Her fox made a tut-tut sound, and a slew of images ran through her mind. All those nights running through the Arizona desert alone. All the times she'd turned down offers to join social occasions at Twin Moon Ranch and stared out at the mesas from the porch of her empty house. All the tossing and turning in bed, trying to get to sleep.

Okay, so Jake wasn't the only one with some ghosts rattling around in his head. But now that she had her mate, the world seemed to have slowed down to a more comfortable pace with a much friendlier vibe.

She looked over and found Jake tipping his head back, testing the sea breeze. Relishing the peace, inside and out. When Jake opened his eyes, he smiled at her — a huge, from-the-heart smile — and pulled her to his side. Those possessive shifter instincts were taking over again, and honestly? Ella didn't mind in the least.

Boone murmured something to Kale and rocked him in his arms as he walked around.

"And you guys said my pacing was bad," Cruz muttered, coming up with Jody.

"Pacing has no purpose. This does. Now be quiet and let my baby sleep."

"Can it be that Boone has finally grown up?" Kai said.

Boone shook his head. "Matured, like a good wine. Now, hand me that rattle, dumbass."

Matured. That was the right word, Ella decided. They weren't much older or much different at the core. They'd all just grown into new roles.

Silas and Cassandra appeared at the edge of the lawn and walked over, hand in hand, further proof of how far the shifters of Koa Point had come. Silas, who'd always been the definition of reserved, broody dragon, wore a huge smile. He looked ten years younger and a hundred times more relaxed than she'd ever seen him. Which was amazing because *Silas* and *relax* were two words that rarely appeared in one sentence unless it was, *Hey, Silas, when are you finally going to relax?*

Well, *finally* had come. Ella took a deep breath. For her and Jake too.

"What?" Jake whispered as everyone called their greetings to the happy couple.

Ella tried gulping away the lump in her throat, but it refused to budge. "I just can't believe it all worked out."

Jake pulled her closer and cupped her face, running his coarse thumbs over her cheeks. "I can."

She took a deep breath. Good old Jake, hanging on to hope even when she had given up. The man was a born shifter with his unshakable faith in love.

Destiny, her fox whispered.

She hugged him then turned to the hubbub behind her. Everyone was laughing, joking, and talking at the same time. Hunter slapped Silas on the back. Dawn admired Cassandra's dress. Boone held up little Kale, and Tessa straightened Kai's thin black tie while Silas and Cassandra made their rounds.

"Looking good, McBride," Silas said, shaking his hand warmly.

Ella's smile stretched. Yeah, her mate looked good, all right.

"Feeling good," Jake said, glancing at Ella. *Thanks to my mate.*

Silas started giving Ella his usual gruff smack on the shoulder. But then he paused, muttered, "Oh, what the heck," and gave her a peck on the cheek. "Am I allowed to do this now?"

Ella laughed, and that lump in her throat finally eased. "Maybe on special occasions."

Everyone chuckled and beamed — Ella, most of all. Could it really be this easy to settle into her own skin? All her life, she'd fought to prove herself. She was proud of that too, but it felt good just to be herself and loosen up a bit.

"Sorry to have delayed the big day," Jake said.

Cassandra just shrugged. "No big deal."

"No big deal? It's your wedding!" Ella sputtered.

Cassandra laughed. "Our very small, friends-and-family-only wedding, just the way we wanted it. The date is easy to change when it's just us."

"We really wanted you to be here for it," Silas added.

"Like I said." Cassandra nodded. "Friends and family." She stressed the last word and winked at Jake.

"And speaking of wanting you to be here—" Silas started.

Cassandra shook her head and rolled her eyes. "There he goes, talking business again."

Silas put his hands up. "Only part business. I wanted to ask you two to stay. I mean, really stay. To join our clan."

"Pack," Boone murmured, correcting Silas as he always did.

Silas ignored him, as *he* always did, and everyone gathered around to hear his words.

"Ella has always been part of our clan. Jake fits right in too, and we'd love for you to join us. You can live at the plantation house. Maybe fix it up. Go on helping us with security. That need hasn't changed. Of course, you don't have to pretend to be honeymooners anymore."

"Ha. The pretending part stopped a while ago." Kai laughed.

Boone grinned. "I have to say, that was pretty fun."

Ella shook her finger at the wolf. "I'd deck you if you weren't holding a baby, Hawthorne."

She was only joking, of course. And honestly, she did feel like a honeymooner. She was that giddy, that overwhelmed by love.

"Hey, we were right about you two being perfect together, weren't we?" Boone said.

That, she had to give him.

"You mean..." Jake said, looking from Boone to Kai and then Hunter.

"Yeah," she sighed. "Seems like the boys were playing matchmaker more than we thought. I'm not sure whether to deck them or let them off easy this time."

Jake mulled it over for a minute then shrugged. "Maybe we'll let them off easy — just this one time." He did give the others a firm look that managed to say *thanks* and *never mess with my mate* at the same time.

Tessa nodded eagerly. "It would be great to have you here."

"Yeah," Jody chimed in. "You could help us keep these guys in line."

Ella's chest expanded in a huge sigh. God, it felt good to be asked. Her first instinct was to jump at the opportunity, but when she really thought it through...

She looked at Jake, whose eyes said it all. Living on Maui with the group of people who understood them best would be great, but the desert Southwest called to them both.

"It's a great offer..." Jake started.

"A really great offer," she rushed to add.

Silas tilted his head. "But?"

Ella bit her lip. How to explain? "We'd love it. Really love it. But there's this little house way out on the edge of a ranch... Thousands of acres of open country..."

Silas chuckled. "Enough space for a couple of freshly mated foxes to roam, huh?"

She nodded quickly. She loved Koa Point, but she loved Twin Moon Ranch as well. Jake would love the ranch too. The peace. The solitude. They would have steady jobs patrolling the vast ranch in a landscape that had been in their blood since birth, and they'd have time together.

A lifetime together. Her fox gave a dreamy sigh.

"Can we visit?" she asked when the breeze shifted, carrying the scent of everything that made Koa Point so special. Flowers. The ocean. Good friends.

"As often as you like."

"Hey, you can stay at Pu'u Pu'eo," Kai said. "Now that we've decided not to sell the property, I mean. I can't believe we ever thought about letting it go."

Ella made a face. "Especially not to someone like Goode. I still can't believe he tracked us to that property."

Kai frowned. "I guess we're not the only ones to have done some detective work. We're already in the process of getting the deed changed so that doesn't happen again."

"Goode," Jake snorted. "Some name."

Ella shook her head, still finding it all hard to believe. Over the past week, Kai and Silas had been busy investigating to get to the bottom of that. Goode was one of many aliases the liger had used. Weapons dealers knew him as Geoff LeBonn, as Kai had discovered. Either way, he was the very man Jake's buddy Hoover had suspected. As a private contractor with shady contacts, Goode had exploited human suffering for personal profit in war-torn regions around the world. Moira had probably rubbed her hands in glee when she'd connected with Goode, the perfect man to do her dirty work. Moira wanted revenge on the shifters of Koa Point, while Goode wanted revenge on Jake for the "crime" of inadvertently derailing a profitable deal.

That's the bastard! Did you get him? She'd heard Hoover bark over the phone when Jake had called two days back.

Oh, we got him, all right, her inner fox hummed.

Kai and Silas had arranged for some contacts on the mainland to follow up on what Ella had learned to ensure Goode's illegal operations were shut down — the weapons deals, the drug deliveries, and the sex-trafficking schemes. Those women had been freed, and the remaining members of Jake's unit could finally breathe easy and grieve for their fallen friends with a measure of peace.

Jake nodded crisply. "I just wish we could have gotten him sooner."

Ella nearly said *I wish we had gotten Moira too,* but this wasn't the time or place. Neither was it time to kick herself for assuming Goode had anything to do with a group of unrelated feline shifters Silas was planning to meet with soon. Instead, she took Jake's hand and held it tightly. "No looking back, McBride. Just forward."

He cracked into a faint smile and nodded. "Forward sounds good to me."

"Speaking of which..." Cassandra cleared her throat deliberately. "I have something to look forward to. Real soon." She turned to Silas. "Are you having second thoughts, or are you ready to get this wedding started?"

Silas laughed — a loose, happy sound Ella had never heard coming from him before. "Bet your ass, I am."

Everyone laughed, and Tessa and Jody scurried around with pink, yellow, and white garlands. Every person got one, with a deluxe version for Cassandra.

"Oh! It's beautiful," the bride exclaimed, ducking for Tessa to loop a lei around her neck and place a lush crown of flowers on her head.

"Dawn made those," Jody explained. "The one I tried was a disaster."

"It's perfect," Cruz growled, touching the bunched-up amateur lei he put on.

"This one's for you, and you, and you..." Tessa said, distributing one to each person.

Jake nudged Ella, and she nodded. "Presents. Right. We have one for you."

"No presents necessary." Silas looked at Cassandra with shining eyes. "We have everything we want. Everything we need."

Ella knew how he felt, but she plunged on. "Well, call it a bonus."

She looked at Jake, and he drew the opal from his pocket and held it out for all to see.

For a moment, everyone went quiet. Then Kai whistled. "Holy..."

"...shit." Boone finished.

Nina stuck her elbow in his ribs. "Baby ears, Boone."

"Sorry. Holy sheet?"

The others stared in wonder. They'd all known about the stone that had given Jake the strength to fight Goode, but Ella had insisted on keeping it close to her mate while he recovered. Now that he was back to full strength, it was time to do the right thing.

"The Keystone," Cassandra whispered. "Is that really it?"

Ella didn't have to answer — not when the rumbling undercurrent of energy around the opal pulsed.

"The stone that gave the others their power," Silas said.

The stone that gave Jake power too. Ella whispered a silent *thank you* to destiny one more time.

"Wait," Tessa murmured, pulling an emerald necklace out from under her blouse. The green glowed brighter — and brighter still when Nina shifted the baby in her arms to reveal her ruby necklace.

"Wow." The ruby was glowing just as brightly.

"It's really true," Dawn breathed, pulling out an amethyst.

When Jody held out a sapphire and Cassandra cupped the diamond around her neck, Ella held her breath.

"The Spirit Stones. All six," Cassandra whispered.

A beam of light glinted off the diamond and shone across the center of the circle they had formed.

"Wow," Kai whispered as a beam of green light crossed the first.

More rays shot out as the rest of the Spirit Stones came to life. Each of the gems emitted its own beam of light, while the mosaic of colors within the opal sparkled and shone back.

"I'm not the only one who feels that, right?" Jody whispered.

Ella shook her head slowly. She felt it, all right. Heat, seeping into her body. Power. Energy.

Jake's throat bobbed, but his hand remained steady under the opal. "What is that?"

"It's like the legends say . . ." Silas said in a hush.

The intersecting beams of light glowed brighter and brighter while the air vibrated with power — power that reached out and swirled around them. Ella's cheeks heated, and she found herself inhaling deeply. Standing taller, straighter. Holding her arms out slightly, soaking in that sense of power. Even little

Keiki looked on, purring madly from her perch on Hunter's broad shoulder.

"Now that's more like what I expected when the Spirit Stones were united," Boone said in an uncharacteristically awed voice.

Silas swung his hand slowly through the beams of light, shaking his head in wonder.

Ella closed her eyes. The sensation coursing through her was like a drug. She felt powerful. Invincible, even. Ready to take on any foe.

Her fox lashed its tail from side to side. *Bring 'em on. Anyone. Everyone. We can stop any enemy, any time.*

It was amazing. Intoxicating. Almost frightening to feel that mystical power.

"Whoa," Cassandra murmured, slowly closing her hand around the diamond. The beam of white light faded, and one by one, the others followed suit until all that was left was a faint thrum of power.

"Can I just say, I'm glad the bad guys don't have that?" Boone murmured in the silence that ensued.

Jake closed his hand, looking as startled as the rest, and handed the opal to Silas. "Like I said, a present."

Silas stared, and Ella nodded. Yes, Jake meant it. The Keystone belonged at Koa Point with the other Spirit Stones. She and he had even driven to the roadside stand to question the woman who had sold Jake the puzzle box, but the woman was gone.

No idea where she went, the man at the lunch truck had said. *She was only here that one day. Never before, never since.*

Destiny, Ella's fox had whispered, awed.

She took a deep breath, thinking it over. Maybe destiny had been on her side longer than she'd thought.

"You're serious," Silas whispered, dumbstruck.

Jake cracked a little smile, trying to keep things light. "I am keeping the box it came in."

"But this..." Silas started.

Jake tipped his head toward Ella. "Got all I want. All I need."

Ella half expected Boone to wisecrack or Silas to make one of his usual, measured replies. But neither said a word. Slowly, Silas accepted the Keystone and cupped it in his hands.

Everyone went quiet — dead quiet — and Ella could sense the emotions spinning around. Relief at finding what they had sought for so long. Respect for Jake, and for the opal's power to magnify the effect of the Spirit Stones. And maybe even a little nervousness, because possessing that kind of power came with huge responsibility.

Silas nodded gravely. "So much power. Almost too much power." But then his gaze went to baby Kale, sleeping peacefully on Boone's shoulder, and little Luna in Nina's arms.

"Maybe just enough power," Jake said quietly. "Just in case."

Ella followed his gaze to the babies — so helpless, so innocent. No one actually mentioned Moira, but Ella could tell the she-dragon was on everyone's mind. Would Moira's spite for the shifters of Koa Point ever abate? Would she hire another mercenary or strike in person someday? Or would she finally give up and leave them in peace?

Ella looked at Jake, and he immediately squeezed her hand. *If we survived the liger, we can survive anything.*

She nodded slowly. Goode had been an especially formidable foe — one whose motives overlapped with Moira's. At least he was out of the equation for good. Moira was still at large, but the shifters of Koa Point had won again. Ella and Jake would stay for as long as necessary, and even after they moved to Arizona, they could fly in at the drop of a hat to help.

She breathed deeply, taking in the gently swaying palms and the circle of her closest friends. Life was full of beauty, but there was evil out there as well. The shifter world was rife with centuries-old conflicts and enemies who had strayed close to this peaceful sanctuary time and again. So, yes. *Just in case* was right. The power of the united Spirit Stones would make the already powerful shifters of Koa Point nearly unassailable.

But just in case. . .

She looked at the Keystone, then Silas. *Keep it. No one can protect it better than you can, and no one can put its power to better use if needed.*

Silas looked at Jake, and suddenly, their roles were reversed. Jake was the generous alpha, and Silas, the man uncertain about the future. "You're sure?"

"Absolutely sure."

Silas took a deep breath. "Well, then. I think it might be best to lock this away."

Cassandra nodded vigorously. "Definitely. Now, get moving. I have a wedding to get to."

That broke the ice and brought out the smiles again. Silas gave Jake the heartiest handshake Ella had ever witnessed, communicating with more than words. Then Silas left Cassandra with a kiss, heading for his house and the hidden lair he kept such treasures in.

"So, Arizona, huh?" Dawn asked.

Jake looked at Ella with a secret smile. "Arizona is perfect."

Boone nodded immediately, but Cruz muttered, "Arizona? No water, man."

Ella raised a hand and swept it over an imaginary view, replacing the lush slopes of Maui with a vision of a huge, open landscape with red rocks, breathtaking canyons, and majestic purple mountains. She and Jake could lope along valley floors, climb mesas, count stars. How could she put all that into words?

Very simple, her fox said. *Home.*

"Not much water, but lots of space," she said, leaving it at that.

Boone went a little dreamy-eyed himself. "Twin Moon Ranch is a pretty great place."

Cruz looked at them as if they were crazy, but Jody gave Ella a thumbs-up. "It sounds great."

Kai sighed. "So we're back where we started. Well, not entirely," he added, shooting Jake and Ella a grin. "But we still need someone to fix up the plantation house and to help with security around here."

Jake put up his hands. "We'll stay as long as you need to find someone."

"The question is, who?"

"The Hoving brothers," Boone immediately replied.

"The three of them?" Kai looked skeptical. "Will that be enough?"

"They're shifters," Boone said. "And they're brothers, so they won't fall in love with each other overnight." He looked at Ella and Jake with a cheeky grin.

I fell in love with Jake a long time ago, Ella nearly pointed out. *I've waited for my mate for so long.*

She closed her eyes, not sure whether to erase the loneliness and despair from her memories or hang on to them to appreciate her mate even more.

Appreciate my mate even more, her fox cooed as Jake pulled her into a hug.

"There they go again," Boone sighed before Nina play-smacked him.

"Like you were any better when we got together, wolf."

Boone leaned down to kiss his mate, and the moment stretched out. In fact, everyone went a little dreamy-eyed until Kai returned to the subject.

"The Hoving brothers would be perfect. And they're about to get out of the service, right?"

"Who's about to get out of the service?" Silas asked, back at his mate's side in record time.

"The Hoving brothers."

Silas groaned. "Did you hear about what they got up to last week?"

Ella leaned closer. She hadn't heard about that part, but then again, the Hoving brothers — a trio of young, cocky guns in the shifter world — had always been in and out of trouble.

Kai scratched his head. "Maybe it would be better to bring them in. They can keep an eye on the property, and we can keep an eye on them."

Silas rolled his eyes. "There's someone else I've had in mind. A shifter who would be perfect for the job. Someone who thinks before they act."

"Who?" Kai asked as everyone looked up.

The breeze shifted, stirring Cassandra's hair, and Silas immediately got that distracted, *I'm so in love with my mate* look. "That's a long story — for another time. Right now, I have a wedding to get to."

As if on cue, the intercom to the front gate crackled, and a chipper voice boomed out.

"Hello? Anyone there? Is this contraption even on? Yoo-hoo..."

Dawn laughed. "Lily. She still hasn't figured that thing out."

"Hello?" Lily shouted. "Can you hear me?"

"Come on in," Hunter said, hitting the remote for the gate.

Everyone turned to the driveway expectantly, and a battered old Nissan pulled into view with Lily waving madly from the driver's seat. The moment she parked the vehicle, she leaped out and rushed forward, making her colorful mu'umu'u sway around her generous curves.

"Well, get moving," Lily called to the bald pastor exiting the car behind her — a man in a starched white shirt and black suit who could have stepped out of a history book's chapter on missionaries who'd come to Maui a century earlier. "We have a wedding, you know."

Lily oohed and aahed over Cassandra's dress, kissed Dawn on both cheeks, and smooched Hunter three times — right cheek, left cheek, right cheek — finishing with a wink. Then she ran over and engulfed Ella in a warm hug just like Georgia Mae used to do.

"Oh, sweetheart. I'm so happy for you. And you," Lily added, pulling Jake down for a peck on the cheek. "Lucky girl." She winked at Ella. "Lucky man, too."

Luckiest man on earth, Jake's eyes agreed.

Luckiest girl on earth, Ella wanted to add. Luckier than she could fathom sometimes. She touched the silver necklace

Jake had found and returned to her. Her mother and Brian never got this moment, but their love would live on in her.

Lily hooked Cassandra in one elbow and Silas in the other and started marching them toward the beach. "Now, about that wedding. Ready, Ernie?"

When the wind blew the pastor's hat off, Cruz snapped it out of the air, startling the wits out of the poor man. Cruz handed it back with an amused, tiger grin. Ella followed closely, wondering about Lily for the hundredth time. How much did she know about shifters? And could the woman be descended from Hawaiian royalty? She had a way of taking charge of every situation while spreading good cheer.

"That woman is a tornado," Jake murmured as everyone fell into step behind Lily.

"I heard that, young man," Lily chirped. "You now owe me a dance — if that woman of yours lets me."

Ella laughed. Lily, she would allow one dance with Jake. But any other woman — no way.

"Oh my gosh," Cassandra exclaimed the moment they came into view of the beach.

"Wow." Ella stopped. She wasn't usually one for flowers but, damn. A row of bouquets led to an archway woven with fragrant white flowers — an arch just big enough for two lucky lovers to stand beneath. In the background, shallow water glittered in brilliant turquoise, and beyond that stretched the pure blue of the sky.

"You like it?" Tessa clapped in excitement. "We worked on it all morning."

"It's gorgeous," Cassandra breathed.

Silas looked pretty wowed too, and Lily had to usher both of them under the arch. Then she hustled the pastor into position and gave him a firm nod.

"Hit it, Ernie."

Not many shifters got married because shifter mating was forever, and human ceremonies... Well, not all of them represented ties as deep. Cassandra had initially joked that the primary purpose of the wedding was to stop local hopefuls from chasing after Silas, but it was clear how much the ceremony meant to her. Even Ella had to sigh at the emotions the classic wedding scene set off.

Are you thinking what I'm thinking? Jake asked, whispering into her mind. *Second chance, I mean?*

She smiled. Officially, she and Jake were married — they'd said *I do* in the rushed wedding on Oahu. Of course, that had all been for the sake of a ruse. But this time, they got to enjoy what it meant. The mating scars on her neck tingled as she looked at her mate.

Married and *mated. How lucky can a girl get?* she replied just as the pastor started the ceremony.

"Dearly beloved. . ."

Everyone hurried into place, forming little rows. Kai and Tessa stood on the right, beaming and holding hands. Ella and Jake stood behind them, while Hunter and Dawn took the left, and Cruz and Jody formed a second row. Nina and Boone stood at the back, rocking the babies and looking as spellbound as everyone else.

Ella looked around, biting her lip. She was part of that group in every way — no longer the odd woman out, but a woman standing firmly beside her mate. Her husband. Her hero.

"Pinch me," she whispered when the pastor started getting to the vows.

Jake grinned and pinched himself instead.

"Do you, Silas Llewellyn. . ." the pastor began.

Ella substituted Jake's name, then her own, mostly following along, but drifting away at times. She couldn't really focus on anything but her mate or how lucky she was. Jake had survived. He was hers. She was his.

Forever, her fox added in a giddy voice.

"To have and to hold. . ."

Jake squeezed her hand, telegraphing something like, *Oh, I'll hold you all right. For the rest of my life.*

"For richer, for poorer. . ."

She pictured the old blacksmith's house way out on the edge of Twin Moon Ranch, with its squeaky old windmill and west-facing porch. It had been a nice place to live over the past few months, but it would be even better with Jake there. Watching blazing Arizona sunsets, patrolling the ranch, writing a new chapter of their lives.

"In sickness and health..."

She squeezed Jake's hand harder. They'd already survived the *sickness* part, and something told her they had many happy, healthy years ahead.

One of the babies cooed, and she peeked over.

Our mate would make a great dad, her fox sighed.

Ella took a deep breath. Jake would, but man. She would need some time to get her head around that one. Good thing they didn't have to rush.

"I now pronounce you..."

Ella blinked a few times, trying not to get too far ahead of herself. She nearly missed throwing her flowers on time, so lost was she in Jake's deep blue eyes.

Everyone cheered, and it felt like they were cheering for her. And in a way, they were. Every couple beamed and clapped and hugged, celebrating the love that was evident all around.

"I love you," Ella whispered, facing Jake.

He clasped both her hands and drew her in for a deep, lingering kiss.

"Love you too, my mate." He said it like he'd grown up with the shifter concept of eternal love.

"I get you forever," she whispered. Did Jake really understand that?

Jake grinned. "Forever is the best part, Kitt."

He kissed her again, and she lost track of everything but the voice of her fox, murmuring inside.

Forever... and ever... and ever.

Sneak Peek: Aloha Shifters: Pearls of Desire

A new *Aloha Shifters* series coming soon! Maui is about to get hotter with this exciting new series of suspenseful paranormal romance you won't want to miss. If you enjoyed **Jewels of the Heart**, you'll love **Pearls of Desire**!

Connor Hoving and his band of shifter brothers are looking to leave trouble behind when they move to Maui, but destiny has a few tricks up her sleeve. Join these sexy shifter heroes as fate confronts them with challenging new obstacles, vengeful enemies, and true love worth living - and dying - for.

Book 1: Rebel Dragon - coming April 2018! Book 2: Rebel Bear - coming May 2018! Book 3: Rebel Lion - coming June 2018! Book 4: Rebel Wolf - coming Fall 2018! Book 5: Rebel Alpha - coming Fall 2018!

Make sure you're subscribed to Anna Lowe's **newsletter** to be the first to hear the release date for this thrilling new ALOHA SHIFTERS series. Visit www.annalowebooks.com today to subscribe and explore free bonus materials available to you there.

Books by Anna Lowe

Aloha Shifters - Jewels of the Heart

Lure of the Dragon (Book 1)

Lure of the Wolf (Book 2)

Lure of the Bear (Book 3)

Lure of the Tiger (Book 4)

Love of the Dragon (Book 5)

Lure of the Fox (Book 6)

The Wolves of Twin Moon Ranch

Desert Hunt (the Prequel)

Desert Moon (Book 1)

Desert Wolf: Complete Collection (Four short stories)

Desert Blood (Book 2)

Desert Fate (Book 3)

Desert Heart (Book 4)

Desert Yule (a short story)

Desert Rose (Book 5)

Desert Roots (Book 6)

Sasquatch Surprise (a Twin Moon spin-off story)

Blue Moon Saloon

Perfection (a short story prequel)

Damnation (Book 1)

Temptation (Book 2)

Redemption (Book 3)

Salvation (Book 4)

Deception (Book 5)

Celebration (a holiday treat)

Shifters in Vegas

Paranormal romance with a zany twist

Gambling on Trouble

Gambling on Her Dragon

Gambling on Her Bear

Serendipity Adventure Romance

Off the Charts

Uncharted

Entangled

Windswept

Adrift

Travel Romance

Veiled Fantasies

Island Fantasies

visit www.annalowebooks.com

About the Author

USA Today and Amazon bestselling author Anna Lowe loves putting the "hero" back into heroine and letting location ignite a passionate romance. She likes a heroine who is independent, intelligent, and imperfect – a woman who is doing just fine on her own. But give the heroine a good man – not to mention a chance to overcome her own inhibitions – and she'll never turn down the chance for adventure, nor shy away from danger.

Anna loves dogs, sports, and travel – and letting those inspire her fiction. On any given weekend, you might find her hiking in the mountains or hunched over her laptop, working on her latest story. Either way, the day will end with a chunk of dark chocolate and a good read.

Visit AnnaLoweBooks.com

Made in the USA
Coppell, TX
29 November 2020

42428662R00132